'Can you hear me, *mademoiselle*?'

'Her name is Gigi.' The curly-haired brunette crouched down opposite him and supplied the name helpfully.

He was in Montmartre, in a shabby, past-its-use-by-date cabaret, with a cast of showgirls whose home cities ranged from Sydney to Helsinki to London—hardly any of them were actually French. Of *course* her name was Gigi.

He didn't believe it for a second.

As if sensing his scepticism, she swept up her thick golden lashes with astonishing effect. A pair of blue eyes full of lively intelligence above angular cheekbones met his. Grew round, startled, and bluer than blue.

The colour of the water in the Pechora Sea.

He should know—he'd just flown in from it.

She sat up on her elbows and fixed him with those blue eyes.

'*Qui êtes-vous?* Who are you?'

His question exactly.

He straightened up to assert a little dominance over her and settled his hands lightly on his lean muscled hips.

'Khaled Kitaev,' he said simply.

There was _____ 't take his eyes off _____ and, and when sh_____ at he wanted_____

Lucy Ellis creates over-the-top couples who spar and canoodle in glamorous places. If it doesn't read like a cross between a dozen old fairytales you half know and a 1930s romantic comedy, it's not a Lucy Ellis story. Come and read a rambling exposition on her books at lucy-ellis.com and drop her a line.

Books by Lucy Ellis

Mills & Boon Modern Romance

A Dangerous Solace
Pride After Her Fall
The Man She Shouldn't Crave
Innocent in the Ivory Tower

What Every Woman Wants

Untouched by His Diamonds

Visit the Author Profile page at
millsandboon.co.uk for more titles.

CAUGHT IN HIS GILDED WORLD

BY
LUCY ELLIS

Published in Great Britain 2015
by Mills & Boon, an imprint of Harlequin (UK) Limited,
Eton House, 18-24 Paradise Road, Richmond, Surrey, TW9 1SR

© 2015 Lucy Ellis

ISBN: 978-0-263-24942-2

Printed and bound in Spain
by CPI, Barcelona

CAUGHT IN HIS GILDED WORLD

Gigi is for you, Mum.

CHAPTER ONE

'GIGI, GET DOWN from there. You're going to break your neck!'

Suspended two metres in the air, gripping the stage curtain between the tensed toes of her feet and using her slender muscled arms to propel herself upwards, Gigi ignored the commentary and made quick work of scaling the curtains alongside the four-metre-high fish tank. It was the same tank in which she would be swimming tonight, in nothing more than a G-string and a smile, with two soporific pythons: Jack and Edna. That was if she didn't get fired first.

The ladder, which would have made this easier, had been folded away, but she was used to shimmying up ropes. She'd been doing it from the age of nine in her father's circus. The velvet stage curtains were a doddle in comparison.

Now for the hard part. She grabbed hold of the side of the tank with one hand and swung a leg over, straddling the ledge and locking herself in place.

There was an audible sigh from below.

When Susie had yelled, 'Kitaev's in the building—front of house, stage left,' pandemonium had broken loose. While the other girls had reached for their lipstick and yanked up their bra straps, Gigi had eyed the tank and, remembering its superb view once you were up there, hadn't hesitated.

Susie had been right on the money, too. Down below, among the empty tables and chairs, deep in conversation with theatre management, was the man who held their future in his powerful hands, surrounded by an entourage of thugs.

Gigi's eyes narrowed on those thugs. She guessed when you were the most hated man in Paris it helped to have minders.

Not that he appeared to need them. His back was to the stage but she could tell his arms were folded because his dark blue shirt was plastered across a pair of wide, power-ful shoulders and a long, equally sculpted torso.

The man looked as if he broke bricks with a mallet for a living, not cabarets.

'Gigi, Gigi, tell us what you can see? What does he look like?'

Big, lean and built to break furniture.

And that was when he turned around.

Gigi stilled. She'd seen pictures of him on the internet, but he hadn't looked like *that*. No, the photographs had left that part out… The *I've just stepped off a boat from a nineteenth-century polar expedition, during which I hauled boats and broke ice floes apart with my bare hands* part.

A beard as dark and wild as his hair partially obscured the lower portion of his face, but even at this distance the strong bone structure, high cheekbones, long straight nose and intense deep-set eyes made him classic-film-star gor-geous. His thick, glossy and wavy inky hair was so long he'd hooked some of it back behind his ears.

He looked lean and hungry and in need of civilising—and why that should translate into a shivery awareness of her own body wasn't something Gigi wanted to investigate right now as she wobbled, gripping the side of the tank.

Not when she had to talk to him and make him listen.

He wasn't going to listen. He looked as if he would *devour* her.

Self-preservation told Gigi that a smart girl would shimmy back down the curtain and mind her own business.

'What's happening?' called up Lulu, who clearly wasn't able to mind her own business either, because she had climbed onto an upturned speaker below and was tugging on Gigi's ankle.

'I don't know,' Gigi called back. 'Give me a minute—and stop pulling at me, Lulu Lachaille, or I really will fall.'

Chastened, Lulu let go, but there was an answering hum of protest from below.

'You're not a monkey, G. Get down!'

'She thinks she's made of rubber. If you fall, Gigi, you won't bounce!'

'Gigi, tell us what you can actually *see*! Is it really him?'

'Is he as gorgeous as he looks in all the photos?'

Gigi rolled her eyes. At least Lulu understood that this man was not going to take his winnings seriously. But the other girls—poor fools—didn't see it that way. They were all operating under the belief that a rich guy in want of entertainment would scoop up a lucky showgirl and whisk her away to a life of unlimited shopping.

Probably alerted by all the noise, Kitaev looked up.

His attention shot to the aquarium so fast she barely had time to think. Certainly it was too late to draw herself back behind the curtain.

His gaze fastened on her.

It was like being slammed into a moving object at force. There was a buzzing in Gigi's ears and suddenly her balance didn't seem as reliable as it had been a moment ago.

She made a little sound of dismay as her belly slipped a few notches from her holding place atop the aquarium.

He was looking up at her now, as if *she* was what he had come to see.

Gigi slipped another inch and grappled for purchase.

Then two things happened at once.

He frowned, and Lulu gave an extra-hard tug on her ankle.

Gigi knew the moment she lost her balance because there was nothing she could do to save herself other than prepare for the fall. And with a little gasp she came tumbling down.

CHAPTER TWO

IT WAS POSSIBLE Khaled would never have known he owned this little piece of Montmartre if someone had not got hold of a list of Russian-owned properties in Paris and published them. Apparently it was fine to buy up significant real estate in the Marais and down south on the Riviera, but touch one of Paris's cabarets and lo and behold you were the most hated man in the city.

Not that Khaled paid attention to what other people thought of him. He'd learned that lesson many years ago, as the son of a Russian soldier who had destroyed his mother's life and brought shame on her family.

Growing up among people who shunned him had formed on him a tough hide, along with the ability to use his fists—although nowadays he was more likely to use his power and influence in a fight—and the wherewithal to take nothing personally.

'Emotional detachment' a woman he'd briefly dated had called it. All skill, but no heart.

Detachment had served him well. Wallowing in emotion probably would have got him killed before he was twenty in the part of the world he came from. He had grown up fast and hard and had survived because of it. Then he had flourished in the bear pit that was the Moscow business world. He knew how to get what he wanted and he didn't let sentiment cloud his reasoning.

What made him a bad bet for a woman looking to nest sent the stock prices of his companies regularly soaring. Not that he was uninterested in women. He had a healthy interest in the species—although the turnover had recently stopped. It wasn't down to emotional emptiness, or an absence of libido, but sheer boredom at the lack of challenge.

He was a hunter. It was intrinsic to his nature to take up a scent, to track, to chase, to make the kill.

Then he got bored.

He had been bored for a long time. Months now.

Then he looked up.

What in *hell* was that?

When a man stepped inside one of Paris's famous cabarets he was primarily looking to see that most legendary of creatures: a Parisian showgirl.

Long-legged, alluring, topless...

That wasn't what he was looking at.

Granted, he'd been living in tents, yurts and huts for the past six weeks, bathing in rivers, eating out of cans and off the carcasses of what they could kill. A hallucination involving a woman might well be the result—although he doubted this was what his mind would come up with. Because he'd swear he'd just got a glimpse of a knobby-kneed Tinker Bell in an animal print leotard, perched on top of the tank in which he'd been told a beautiful semi-naked showgirl would be swimming tonight—with pythons.

Almost before he could account for what he was seeing, the curious apparition vanished as suddenly as she'd appeared, followed by a thump and vague female shrieks.

'Do you want to check that out?' he asked of the two Danton brothers, both of whom were clearly sweating bullets over his unannounced appearance.

Neither man moved.

'The girls are in rehearsal,' said Martin Danton nervously, as if that explained everything.

His security detail looked around, clearly expecting all twenty-four luscious Bluebirds to come can-canning across the empty stage.

'Would you like to see a rehearsal?' Jacques Danton volunteered, catching hold of the shift in male attention eagerly. A little too eagerly.

The two Frenchmen who managed the place were nervous

as cats on a hot tin roof—as well they might be. Although Khaled suspected their nerves were nothing more than a natural response to having their shaky business practices put under the microscope.

'My lawyers will be in touch today,' he informed them calmly. 'I want to take a look at how the place is doing.'

'We're a Parisian institution, Mr Kitaev!' they chorused.

'So the French media have hammered home all week,' he replied, with the same measured calm. 'But it's a business, and I like to know how all my businesses are doing.'

Frankly, he wouldn't be here now if the press hadn't exploded last week with spurious accusations that he was the equivalent of the Russian Army—marching on Paris, ripping up its pretty boulevards and despoiling French culture. Turning their city into Moscow-by-the-Seine.

All because he'd won a cabaret in a card game.

Now, having pretty much run his eye over what was making it difficult for him to move around the city without security, he was ready to organise its disposal.

He had meetings lined up this afternoon, so L'Oiseau Bleu's time was almost up.

There was an interruption as a winsome girl with a mop of dark curls stuck her head through the curtain.

'Jacques…' she whispered.

The older man frowned. 'What is it, Lulu?'

'There's been an accident.'

'What sort of accident?'

'One of the girls has hit her head.'

With a Gallic gesture of acceptance, Jacques Danton muttered something that sounded like, 'Zhee-zhee,' and excused himself, pounding up onto the stage and into the wings.

Khaled's gaze flickered to the empty tank, towering over the stage. He still wasn't sure what it was he'd seen but he was interested in finding out.

He moved and his security team swarmed up onto the stage with him.

'I don't really think this is a good idea,' protested Martin Danton as he mobilised himself behind them, exhibiting the first bit of backbone Khaled had seen in either man.

He and his brother had been managing the cabaret for some fourteen years, according to the records. Managing it into the ground, Khaled suspected.

He made his way behind the curtains and through a jungle of stage props, stepping over various crates and boxes, and ducking overhanging cords and wires that probably constituted health and safety risks that would close the place down.

When he saw her she was lying sprawled on the stage floor.

Jacques Danton was ignoring her in favour of remonstrating with the little brunette. It had the effect on Khaled that all the mismanagement and blundering about hadn't yet delivered. He shouldered the Frenchman out of the way and went to her aid.

Hunkering down, he discovered that on closer inspection, despite her eyes remaining closed, he could see her delicate eyelids twitching.

His mouth firmed.

Little faker.

Looking up, he judged the height and recognised that although she'd fallen she couldn't have done much damage.

On cue, a clutch of other Lycra-clad, giggling, whispering twenty-something female dancers closed in around him. Khaled had had a similar experience only days ago, in the highlands of the Caucasus with a herd of jeyran gazelles. One minute he'd been naked, waist-deep in a clear stream, the next he'd been surrounded by knobby-kneed deer intent on drinking their fill.

He looked around to note that his security team appeared as bemused as he was feeling.

What were they going to do? Tackle them?

Obviously he'd been set up, and this was a stunt to get him backstage. But the girls appeared as harmless as the deer. He looked down at the one gazelle who'd separated herself from the herd. She lay there, unnaturally still, but those eyelids gave her away, twitching at high speed as if she'd attached a jump lead to them.

He pressed back one of the delicate folds. 'Can you hear me, *mademoiselle*?'

'Her name is Gigi.' The curly-haired brunette had crouched down opposite him and supplied the name helpfully.

He was in Montmartre, in a shabby, past-its-use-by-date cabaret, with a cast of showgirls whose cities of origin ranged from Sydney to Helsinki to London—hardly any of them were actually French. Of *course* her name was Gigi.

He didn't believe it for a second.

As if sensing his scepticism, she swept up her thick golden lashes with astonishing effect. A pair of blue eyes full of lively intelligence above angular cheekbones met his. Grew round, startled, and bluer than blue.

The colour of the water in the Pechora Sea.

He should know—he'd just flown in from it.

He watched as the points in her face—a gorgeous Mediterranean nose, a wide pink mouth and a pointed chin, all framed by wild red hair—seemed to coalesce around those same eyes.

His chest felt tight, as if he'd been kicked under the ribs.

She sat up on her elbows and fixed him with those blue eyes.

'Who are you? *Qui êtes-vous?*' Her accent happily butchered the French with the sing-song cadence of Ireland blurred with something a little more international.

Qui êtes-vous?

His question exactly.

He straightened up to assert a little dominance over her and settled his hands lightly on his lean muscled hips.

'Khaled Kitaev,' he said simply.

There was a ripple of reaction.

'Ladies…' he added. But he didn't take his eyes off Red as he calmly offered her his hand, and when she hesitated he leaned in and took what he wanted.

Gigi had been falling professionally since she was nine years old, but that hadn't prevented her flailing backwards and striking her head and her tailbone on the stage boards. She was currently seeing two hands and was not sure which one to take.

'Get up!' Jacques was hissing at her like a goose.

The option was taken out of her hands by Kitaev, who plucked her effortlessly off the ground and deposited her on her feet in front of him. Only the room swayed and her legs weren't co-operating.

It didn't help either that she now found herself in the invidious position of having to tilt her head back even though she was five eleven—because he was *that* big—and he was standing far too close…looking at her.

Boy, oh, boy, the way he was looking at her!

Gigi blinked rapidly to clear her vision.

Sometimes men looked at you as if all they wanted was to see you naked. Gigi accepted this as an occupational hazard even if she hated it. Sometimes they made unwanted and sleazy advances, but she'd learned to combat those too.

This man wasn't doing any of those things. His eyes weren't desperate, greedy, pulling at her admittedly ratty leotard as if seeing her naked was all he cared about.

No, this man's eyes held intent. They said something else entirely. Something no man had ever promised her. He was going to strip her naked and pleasure her body as she'd never been pleasured before. And then he was going to take her job and bin it.

'You can't do that!' Gigi blurted out.

'Do what, *dushka*?' He spoke lazily, in a deep Russian accent, as if he had all the time in the world.

There was a titter among the other girls.

'Whatever it is you have planned…' Gigi's voice trailed off, because it didn't sound as if either of them were talking about the cabaret.

'At the moment,' he responded, with a flicker of something certainly beyond her experience in those dark and distant eyes, 'not much besides lunch.'

The laughter around them drowned out any response—which was just as well, because it didn't take much imagination to see that this man had absolutely no interest in anything here—and Gigi felt her initial frustration build once more.

He didn't care what happened to this place. The other girls didn't care. They *would* care, however, when they didn't have jobs.

But it wasn't just about losing a job. This was her *home*.

The anguish that pulled through Gigi like an undertow was real. It was the only place she had ever felt she really belonged since her mother's sudden death had upended her safe, secure world.

She'd served her time with her father until she'd been able to make her leap across the Channel onto the stage boards of what had seemed then to be a dream job.

Although, to be honest, if you'd asked her last week about her job she would have rolled her eyes and complained about the hours, the pay and the lousy chorie.

The Moulin Rouge, it wasn't.

But this wasn't an average day. This was the day everything she'd stitched together from her earliest life with her mother was threatening to come undone.

Gigi was not going to let that happen. She *couldn't* let it happen.

Besides, this wasn't any ordinary theatre. The most amazing women had danced here. Mistinguett, La Belle Otero, Josephine Baker—even Lena Horne had sung on this stage.

And then there was Emily Fitzgerald. Nobody remembered her—she'd never been famous…just a beautiful chorus girl among many who had danced on this stage for five short years. Her mother.

When she fell pregnant to smooth-talking Spanish showman Carlos Valente she had been forced to return home to her family in Dublin, her Paris dream over. But from the moment she'd been able to stand Gigi had had her feet stuffed into *pointe* shoes, had been pushed in the direction of a stage and raised on stories of the Bluebird in its fabulous heyday.

Of course it hadn't been anything like those stories when she'd landed at its door aged nineteen, but unlike the other girls she knew how truly special L'Oiseau Bleu had once been…and could be again.

She'd been working on the Dantons. She'd been sure she was halfway to getting some improvements made to the routines…

Only now *he* was getting in the way.

At a loss as to where to start, it was then that she remembered she *did* have something that could speak for her. Folded up and stuck down her sports bra.

She tugged it out, sadly crumpled, and smoothed down the single page. It was a printout Lulu had made from a burlesque blog they both followed: *Parisian Showgirl*.

She looked up to find Kitaev was still watching her and had probably got an eyeful of her frayed purple bra. She knew this wasn't looking a whole lot professional, but she hadn't *meant* to come crashing down, she hadn't *meant* for him to come hunting around backstage, and right now all she had was…this. It just happened to be in her bra.

Something close to amusement shifted in those dark, watchful eyes. 'What else do you keep in there?'

His voice was pure Russian velvet, quiet and low-pitched, but a bit like a seismic shift in the earth's plates. You felt it in your bones…and other places.

Gigi experienced a whole body flush and drew herself up stiffly. 'Nothing,' she said uncertainly.

A couple of the girls tittered.

Ignoring them, she held out the page until he took it.

Gigi watched him run a cursory glance over the print. She knew it by heart.

Paris is in revolt over the news that Russian oligarch Khaled Kitaev, one of Forbes' richest men under forty, got lucky in a game of poker.

Kitaev, whose fortune is in oil but who, like most Russian businessmen, seems to have branched out into property and entertainment until his holdings resemble nothing less than the behemoth nervous European business columnists fear will simply devour everything in its path—yes, that Kitaev—has taken possession of one of Paris's famous cabarets.

And this isn't just any theatre, people, it's one of Montmartre's oldest cabarets: L'Oiseau Bleu. Home of the Bluebirds. A charming, old-time cabaret—but for how long?

Judging from the media reaction, it appears the French aren't going to take this one lying down.

His hand closed over the piece of paper and *crunch*—it was nothing more than a small ball in his large fist.

Gigi couldn't help feeling they were all a little like that ball of paper, and just as disposable.

'What do you want to know?'

He made it sound so easy, but she wasn't fooled. His dark eyes had hardened over the course of his cursory glance, and when he raised them there was a warning there.

Gigi told herself they weren't *her* words that she'd handed him. But she wanted him to know that this was the position they were operating from. A little information—even if it was misinformation. The sensible thing to do now would be to ask rationally and politely if he foresaw any major changes to the theatre that were going to affect their jobs.

Only then she noticed the subtle movement of his hard

gaze over her body. He wasn't being obvious but she felt it all the same—and, dammit, her nipples stiffened.

So instead of being reasonable she lost her temper and went for broke. 'We want to know if you've any plans to turn our cabaret into a full-on high-octane version of Le Crazy Horse?'

CHAPTER THREE

MARTIN DANTON MADE a groaning sound.

His brother looked poised to take the little redhead out. Red stood her ground.

'I wouldn't know,' responded Khaled, not taking his eyes off her, 'never having been inside the Crazy Horse.'

He caught the slight eye-roll and the tightening of her lips. His hand tightened around the crumpled ball of spurious invective this young woman had clearly swallowed whole.

'Gigi, *ça suffit*,' interrupted Jacques Danton. *That's enough.*

But she didn't back down. 'I think we have a right to know,' she protested. 'It's *our* jobs.'

He would have been more impressed if he hadn't suspected her boss had put her up to it.

'Your jobs are safe for the moment.' He threw it in because it was accurate—today. Tomorrow, possibly not.

'*Splendide!*' Jacques Danton beamed.

'That's not what I asked,' Red interrupted, and she lifted those lively blue eyes to his.

Not in appeal, he registered, but setting herself against him. Clearly not fooled one bit—unlike her boss.

For a moment he considered the alternative: that this *wasn't* some set-up and that the girl—a lot sharper than the Dantons and, unlike them, willing to take him on—was acting alone.

'We're not a strip club, Mr Kitaev, and it would ruin—'

She took a breath and something like anguish crumpled up her striking features. In the time it took her to compose herself Khaled became interested in what exactly she thought he was ruining for her.

But she shook her head and changed direction. 'Ruin the character of the theatre!'

'I wasn't told the theatre had a *character*.'

More laughter.

She looked around, as if thrown by the lack of support, and unexpectedly his conscience stirred.

'Nobody is going to be asked to take off their clothes,' he said, exasperated. Hell, he didn't know *what* would happen here. Go on as before, bleeding funds, because after the dose he'd had of French spleen over the place only a fool would touch it? He'd be lucky to give it away.

Red, however, seemed to be under the mistaken belief that there was something here worth saving.

'*Voulez-vous, filles?*'

Jacques Danton began clapping his hands at the other dancers and their audience began to break up.

'*Maintenant*, Gigi,' he snapped.

She was clearly torn between doing as she was told and continuing to question him about their jobs, but Khaled could already see she wouldn't stand up to her boss.

Just him.

Which was a first, given that men with a lot more where-withal than this girl—industrialists, Duma members, Moscow gangsters—stepped carefully around him. Then again, those men didn't have her lavender eyes or, frankly, her sexual pull.

She was by no means the most beautiful girl backstage, but she was the only one he couldn't take his eyes off.

Something to do with her bold features and lively eyes, and an innate sensuality she appeared to be entirely unaware of.

Pity she danced here…

Shame he was flying out tomorrow…

Another dancer—the frowning little brunette—had edged up to her. She took Red's hand with a furtive look of disapproval in his direction and tugged her away. Smart girl.

Red…*Gigi*…kept glancing over her shoulder at him before the rest of the dancers swallowed her up.

It was a slender shoulder, as finely designed as the rest of her, and it put him in mind of the Spanish painter Luis Ricardo Falero's amusing, graceful mythological girls. He knew he was done here, and yet he found his eyes following the red pigtails, bouncing amidst the crowd of other girls as the famous Bluebirds vanished into the rabbit warren of corridors.

That evening the dressing room was noisier and more lively than usual before the first performance.

Khaled Kitaev was the sole subject of discussion.

'The rumour is that the Russian supermodel Alexandra Dashkova had herself wrapped in a rug, Cleopatra-style, taken up to his hotel suite in Dubai last month and unrolled before him like war booty.'

This was greeted with various *oohs* and *aahs* and had Gigi hesitating in the act of applying three-ounce lashes to her eyelids.

'No one's got a chance with him, then,' groaned Adele at Susie's announcement, and the cramped dressing room was filled with sighs and grumbles and more speculation.

'C'est vrai.' Solange regarded her breasts with satisfaction, adjusting her diamante-studded costume. 'He's asked for me by name. I'm having a drink with him after the show tomorrow.'

Gigi's hand slipped and the fake lashes ended up partway down her cheek.

'Great,' grumbled Lulu under her breath, leaning forward to pluck the feathered blob from Gigi's cheek and pass it to her. 'Ten to one she'll sleep with him and make the rest of us look easy.' Only being Lulu she didn't actually say *easy*—she mouthed it.

There was a neat little division down the centre of the Bluebirds. The dancers who accepted invitations from the visiting Hollywood A-listers and rock stars who came to

he shows, and those who lined up each night after the last
show for the courtesy bus.

It was something Gigi had organised when a couple of
he girls had complained about not feeling safe leaving the
venue at night, given that the theatre was bumped up against
he red light district, and now the bus was a regular thing.

Gigi and Lulu never missed the bus. Solange took every
nvitation that came her way. Apparently she'd taken this
one too.

Not that there was anything wrong with that, Gigi told
herself. She only cared because it confirmed her worst suspicions about Kitaev's plans for them.

She slapped down the lid on her make-up case.

'Sorry G,' said Leah, obviously alerted by the bang of
Gigi's case and not sounding sorry at all. 'You went to all
that trouble for nothing.'

'Not for nothing,' Lulu rallied back loyally in her defence.
'We all got a good look.'

Too good, thought Gigi fiercely. Any hope that Khaled
Kitaev was going to take ownership of the cabaret seriously
was out of the window. As of now the Bluebird was in serious jeopardy.

And what was it with everyone thinking she'd done it on
purpose? *Sheesh.*

No, she knew all about this man. She had scrolled through
lists of his public holdings on the internet, chased them to
various websites, and was still struggling to make sense of
how he'd made his money.

Initially, it appeared, as an oil trader—but he seemed to
have a finger in a lot of pies. *Shady*, she decided. She had
learned from watching her dad at work that big money was
probably amassed in the same way as her father's smaller
cheats: through the exploitation of someone else.

'So what do you think he's going to do to us?' asked
Trixie, one of the youngest dancers.

Given he'd already honed in on Solange, Gigi had a pretty good idea.

'Do you think he'll try to change things? Maybe fix things up?' Trixie sounded optimistic. 'It might not all be bad, Gigi.'

No, it was probably worse. Gigi hated to disillusion her, but facts had to be faced.

She stood up to face the room.

'Could I have everyone's attention?'

A couple of the girls glanced her way, but the noise level didn't drop.

She raised her voice. 'Can we just try to look at the big picture here—instead of getting into a lather about his sex life?'

The word 'sex' had a few more heads turning and the volume dropping.

'Kitaev owns a string of gambling venues around the world.' Gigi paused to let that sink in. 'Have you thought about what that might mean for us?'

'*Oui,*' said Ingrid, 'a pay-rise.'

There was a ripple of laughter.

'Loosen up, G,' advised another girl, giving her a friendly push.

'She can't—she hasn't been laid in so long I'm surprised she didn't squeak when she fell off that aquarium,' cackled Susie.

'Gigi's just smarting because her little stunt didn't make him single her out,' sang out Mia from across the room.

'Give it up, G,' said Adele. 'Oh, that's right—you never do!'

There was a howl of good-natured laughter.

Gigi knew she needed to get the discussion back on track, because now Susie was wanting to know what the point was of being a showgirl if you didn't take advantage of the perks: rich men.

'The point is no one should date Kitaev,' Gigi interrupted. 'He shouldn't be encouraged!'

The laughter only became more raucous. Even Lulu gave her a rueful look.

He's going to win, thought Gigi a little desperately.

The dressing room door banged open.

'Guess who's just arrived, ladies?' announced Daniela, sparkling in full costume.

There was a twitter of excitement.

'Not Kitaev.'

The twittering died down.

'Girls, its wall-to-wall security and every rich Russian in the city is here—and everyone from Fashion Week seems to have followed them. The media are ten-thick outside. I think I'm going to faint!'

Amidst the shrieks, Lulu adjusted her headdress and said brightly, 'There you go, Gigi. Maybe he's not so bad for business after all.'

'So he's sent his friends?' she grumbled. 'One night does not a week make. We're just a novelty act for a bored, spoilt-for-choice, testosterone-injected, arrogant—'

But now even her best friend had jumped ship and was on her way out, giggling with the other girls, trailing the six-foot feather tail they all had attached to their waists for the first number.

Troubled, Gigi finished attaching her own.

That many customers wasn't to be sneezed at, given they regularly performed to a half-empty theatre, and this had been their worst year yet.

Maybe the other girls saw something she didn't.

Yes, she thought cynically, they saw something, all right. They saw Solange draping her skinny arms around Khaled Kitaev's broad neck and a line of ambitious showgirls asking when was it *their* turn.

Solange was apparently going to have hers, and it firmed Gigi's chin.

The lowest common denominator was not going to save this theatre or their jobs.

Khaled Kitaev didn't care about the cabaret. He had no stake in it. He'd won the thing in a card game. All he cared about was the bottom line. Specifically at the moment that bottom being Solange's, but Gigi could well imagine him cutting a swathe through the other bottoms of the troupe. There were some very shapely bottoms.

Gigi swished her plumage-heavy tail like a haughty lyre-bird and took off after the other girls.

She would see about that.

'Mademoiselle…?'

'Valente.'

'*Mademoiselle*, I'm afraid I cannot give you the information you seek. At the Plaza Athénée we value our guests' right to privacy.'

The concierge gave her that bland smile peculiar to people in his job all over the world. Only somehow the Frenchman managed to add that extra little soupçon of superiority.

Gigi knew her bad accent wasn't helping. She should have brought Lulu along this morning. Lulu was half-French, and her big brown Audrey Hepburn eyes and air of delicate femininity made grown men trip over themselves to help her out. With her propensity to help herself and make a mess of it, Gigi found she was mostly sidelined and all too frequently laughed at.

Still, you could only work with what you'd got, and given she'd left her flat in such a hurry this morning she'd left off her make-up, and with her hair still damp and messy from being dunked in the sink, it wasn't exaggerating to say she currently had the sex appeal of an otter.

'But how am I supposed to reach him?' she tried again.

'*Mademoiselle* could try the telephone.'

'You'll give me his number?'

'*Non*, I would assume that as you are the *friend* you say you are, you will have it.'

'I'm not his friend, exactly,' Gigi prevaricated, and because she had a detestation of lies and subterfuge, having seen the chaos her father left in his wake, she opted for the truth. 'I'm his employee. I'm a showgirl at L'Oiseau Bleu.'

For the first time the concierge looked directly at her instead of addressing that distant spot beyond her shoulder.

'Vous êtes une showgirl?'

She relaxed. Everyone loved a showgirl. It was like carrying a great big shiny key to the city.

'Oui, m'sieur.'

The concierge leaned closer. 'Is it true, then? The barbarian is at the gate?'

What gate? It took Gigi a moment to catch on. She'd forgotten in the other girls' excitement that most of Paris shared her misgivings about the 'foreign usurper'. Giving it her best, *I'm as distressed as you are* look, she manufactured a theatrical sigh. 'I'm afraid so.'

'Dieu sauver la France!' He crossed himself.

Gigi tried not to let her surprise show. Given *she* was the one with her job at risk, it was odd how personally the Parisian in the street was taking the new ownership of L'Oiseau Bleu.

Perhaps if those same people transformed their outrage into actually coming to a show and pushing up box office receipts they'd have a chance of survival. Blaming the newcomer on the scene—even if he *was* a Russian oligarch with questionable intentions—didn't seem quite fair.

But she didn't hesitate to press her advantage—it was one of the few things she had learned from her father that she could use.

'Quite. Now, can I have that room number?'

The concierge looked most sympathetic. *'Non,'* he said.

Gigi didn't push it. She turned around, her shoulders sinking, and as she wondered if she should leave a message for him, which would probably go unread, everything changed.

Khaled Kitaev had just entered the lobby.

He was looking at his phone, which gave her the moment

she needed to pull herself together, although the aggression in his body language should have had her second-guessing her decision even to try this.

Be brave, Gigi, she lectured herself. *You've had more auditions than hot meals. It's just another audition... Only* this was possibly her last chance, and it could all go so horribly wrong.

As he strode towards her she took in the unruly dark hair, the beard that framed his beautiful face and enhanced that whole macho thing he was into.

It was working. Women's heads were turning as if they were EMF devices, picking up on his frequency, and not a few men were looking him up and down as they reconsidered the suits they'd so carefully dressed in this morning.

It took a lot of machismo and confidence to render a pair of trainers, sweat pants and a long grey T-shirt with some indecipherable Cyrillic lettering on it stylish against the luxury of the hotel's interior and its swish inhabitants, but Khaled Kitaev pulled it off. Everyone else just looked wrong.

He was coming right for her.

There was no hiding now.

Think about what you're going to say. Be polite. Be professional.

She took some deep calming breaths.

Have some of your material ready. But don't shove it at him. Be friendly, but formal.

She wasn't sure how she'd manage friendly but formal.

He looked up from his phone and at the concierge. All the nearby hotel staff had leapt to attention. He lowered the phone long enough to ask for two brand-new laptops to be sent up to his suite.

'Landslide?' he growled into the phone. 'There's one a day in that part of the world. Get a bulldozer in there and clear the damn thing.'

Gigi observed this exchange with pulse-raised interest, flinching a little as she watched his hand flatten to its full wingspan dimensions on the desk, so close to her she could have reached out and touched it. But she was glad she didn't when he fired some aggressive Russian into the ear of whoever was on the other end of his call. Maybe now wasn't a good time...

Khaled slammed his hand against the nearest solid surface. He couldn't believe it. *Another* meeting pushed back by the village council. *Another* surveyor's report held up because of a landslide.

He wouldn't put it past the clan elders to plant a stick of dynamite into the escarpment and bring down half the mountain onto the highway below just to damn well spite him. Two years and he was no closer to putting that road in.

No road—no resort.

How many people had he sent into the gorge to explain the benefits a new infrastructure would bring? *Any* infrastructure in a corner of the world where the men still herded sheep on horseback. Always there was the same response: initial agreement, new contracts drawn up and then at the last minute something would interfere.

When he had spoken with the clan council they had taken him to task about his Russian investors and the lack of consultation. Khaled had stood, arms folded, at the back of the low dark room that served as a community hall in the town and refused to react or engage.

All he had seen was the memory of his stepfather's eyes, narrow like slits, as he beat him with a piece of horse tack as if that would make him less another man's son.

Unable to withstand the brutality of the memory, without a word Khaled had walked out into the bright daylight, jumped into his truck and driven out of the valley. His last communication with the council was when he was much further north, flying over the Pechora Sea, inspecting a Kitaev oil platform, and a message had been sent to him via his lawyers.

Where is your home? Where is your wife? Where are your children? When you have these things come to us in the proper way and we will talk.

In other words, *Respect our customs and we'll see it your way.*

Customs... He was a modern man, and he had made his fortune in a modern world—he wasn't entering into that kind of old-world game-playing...

He turned away from the desk, snapping his phone closed, catching his elbow on someone's round, firm...

'Ow!'

He looked down and golden-lashed blue eyes turned up to his like searchlights, complete with a little scowl that brought her fine coppery brows together and formed a knot.

'You...' he said, clearing his throat.

'Yes, me!' Her low-pitched, softly accented voice was like Irish whisky—unexpected in a girl so slight and young. She had one hand clamped over her breast and was tenderly massaging the area, her expression pained.

'Forgive me.' His gaze dipped to what little he could see, given her hand was stashed under her jacket.

When she'd pulled out that bit of libel yesterday she'd flashed a purple bra cup and the swell of a firm milk-pale breast marked on the gentle upper slope by a single dark brown freckle. It was a freckle he'd had on his mind ever since.

Only today she appeared to be wearing some kind of pink T-shirt, high-necked, completely unrevealing, along with jeans and a blue wool jacket.

She'd also ditched the pigtails, and her hair hung heavily over her shoulders—coppery red, long, thick and wavy... messy, if you got down to it. Sexy.

Sexy he didn't need. For one thing, he was signing her pay cheques. Ostensibly. Although he'd seen how much those girls were paid. He'd laid down more on a tie than on her monthly wage.

All the more reason to keep moving…

Which he did.

Gigi watched him walk away from her without another word, as if their encounter had never happened. She tried not to be offended. She'd pretty much expected it would take some effort. After all, she wasn't sexy Solange, offering who knew what? She was woman-on-a-mission Gigi, offering flyers and a presentation.

Not that he knew that. But she guessed he only needed a glance to work out the difference between them.

Nevertheless, she hurried after him, swinging her backpack forward over one shoulder and rummaging inside for the vintage-style flyers she'd brought to show him—evidence of how classy the Bluebird had once been and could be again.

He'd see that she was serious and had done her research, and he might sit down and talk to her.

She was right behind him when there was a whoosh of movement in the air beside her—and for the second time in as many days Gigi found herself on the floor, the stuffing knocked out of her.

CHAPTER FOUR

A MALE VOICE GRUNTED, 'Do not move.'

Gigi didn't think she'd be moving. No, not moving at all. She was too stunned to do anything other than lie there, even once the knee resting on the base of her spine was gone and her arms, which had been pinned to her sides, were once more her own.

She only began to react when she was being hauled—not ungently—to her feet. She swayed as blood rushed back into her head and an arm came around her waist to support her. She staggered, and her nose and forehead banged against a hard male chest. She inhaled faint spicy aftershave and heat.

Gigi edged up her chin and her gaze locked on eyes so lustrously dark it was like being dropped into a hot, dark night.

The world shrank down to his thick, steady heartbeat and her short, rapid breaths.

He was speaking to her, but it was like being underwater. All she could make out was that no one was attacking her and the big male arms clamped around her felt like protection.

Which was when she spotted a gorilla—the same one who had knocked her down—turning out her backpack.

It was a replay of her worst memory.

Her limbs exploded and she desperately tried to free herself.

"That's mine! Give me back my things! You have no right to touch my things!'

She made a hopeless grab for it, but Khaled Kitaev had hold of her elbow.

'Calm down, *dushka*.'

She wasn't going to calm down! The last time she'd had her belongings confiscated she'd had handcuffs slapped on her wrists and spent a night in the cells, thanks to her dad.

She struggled, but his strength was all over hers. Gigi lashed out with her elbow and struck him in the chest. Unlike her own chest there was nothing soft and tender about it—instead there was considerable muscle and definition and she only jarred her shoulder.

'That's enough!'

She stopped flailing long enough for him to release her. She pushed her hair out of her eyes with hands that were shaking uncontrollably. So much for being professional. Both of them.

'Mr Kitaev, do we have a problem?'

The discreet enquiry was made by the concierge she had spoken to earlier. He materialised at her side, every inch the gatekeeper for the wealthy and influential. Gigi's insides turned to liquid.

Khaled saw the effect on Red. She looked as if he was about to throw her to the lions.

'*Nichevo.* No problem. A slight misunderstanding.'

'Yes, sir, these things can happen. But the young lady—'

'Mademoiselle Valente,' said Khaled smoothly, and her name was right there, given he'd just happened to take a look at her file last night, 'is my guest.'

'I see, sir.'

'My security team didn't recognise her and were overzealous. I apologise for the inconvenience to your other guests.'

'Not at all, Mr Kitaev.' But the concierge continued to regard Red with interest.

The look on her face had been comic in its alarm and indecision as she followed this exchange, but now as they both turned their attention her way she visibly pulled herself together.

'That's right,' she said gamely. 'I'm here to speak to him.'

Him being the hotel's highest paying guest.

Khaled fully expected the staff to evaporate, but to

his credit the concierge lingered. 'Are you certain *mademoiselle*?'

The hectic look on her face was ebbing away as she appeared to realise that the hotel management was offering her real assistance and not showing her the door.

She nodded slowly, and added, '*Merci beaucoup,*' with an almost comically sincere look on her face, even as her eyes kept zoning in on her backpack.

Khaled gave it a light shake.

What did she have in there? The Crown Jewels? A nuclear weapon? After her little display, neither would have truly surprised him.

'You're not hurt?' he asked as the hotel staff evaporated back into the luxurious fittings.

'No,' she huffed, looking around as if expecting another attack. 'No thanks to your lunatic friends.'

'Bodyguards.'

She blinked, clearly not familiar with the concept.

'They are employed to look to my safety.'

'Why?'

Why...? Khaled wasn't often asked this question. Usually people were calling him sir and getting out of his way. 'It is common in my line of business.'

'Hmm.' She didn't sound convinced. 'Yes, well, you need to put them on a leash.'

Struggling manfully with a desire to throw back his head and laugh, Khaled murmured, 'I apologise unreservedly. It was an unforgivable breach of your human rights.'

She eyed him suspiciously. 'You don't sound particularly sincere.'

Was she going to argue with him about this too?

'I guess you're having some fun at my expense,' she allowed slowly.

Unexpectedly he remembered the lack of support given to her by the other dancers yesterday, and the laughter that greeted her pronouncements.

'My papa used to say all I needed was a curly wig and a red nose and I'd have a new job.'

He frowned. 'Most fathers think their daughters are princesses.'

Gigi wondered if being seventeen years old and dancing onstage in a costume made of balloons she'd strategically popped with five other girls, until she was virtually down to her little yellow bikini, while her father systematically fleeced the audience had an attendant fairy tale.

'My father raised me to live in the real world,' she said uncomfortably, darting another glance at her backpack. Was he *ever* going to give it back?

Following her gaze, he proffered it. 'I believe this belongs to you?'

She was obviously trying not to appear too eager but she still snatched at it, and clearly couldn't help plastering it to her chest.

'So, does this happen to you all the time? Bodyguards leaping out and knocking people over?'

'You were coming towards me and you'd reached into your bag.'

She frowned. 'Why is that a problem?'

He made a trigger gesture with his hand.

Her frown deepened.

'A gun,' he clarified.

'A *gun*?' Her voice rose. 'They thought I had a *gun*!' This notion was clearly as foreign to her as the French language she was so deliciously butchering with her accent.

A passing couple stared at them and she shut up.

Khaled tried not to smile.

'I really don't see that there's anything funny about this,' she said tightly.

'*Nyet*—nothing funny.'

'I didn't come to shoot you—obviously. I came to speak to you about the cabaret.'

There was an awkward silence as he just looked at her.

She tried again.

'I know it's unorthodox, but I figured as we'd met…'

He folded his arms. 'I remember you lying on the floor.'

Gigi wondered whether, if she'd been lying on the floor right now, he would have stepped over her and kept going. Probably.

She reviewed her options. She'd gone over it with Lulu last night and decided her best hope of success was to bring all the material she'd compiled on the cabaret's star-studded history and her ideas for its future and lay it before him.

Be confident. Make an appeal to his better nature and leave any mention of Solange out of it. The last had been Lulu's firm instruction.

'Do not mention Solange.'

Well, she hadn't. But maybe she hadn't been plain enough.

'It's handy that you remember me,' she said, overly bright. 'You see, I'm spokesperson for the troupe.'

'You don't say?' He glanced at his watch.

She was already losing him.

For the first time Gigi noticed that he looked a bit more disreputable than she remembered him being yesterday, and it was only now she fully focussed on the T-shirt, running shoes and the pair of pricey sweats and what they represented.

'Are you on your way to do some exercise?' she asked, a little desperately.

'Da,' he said with enviable cool, his gaze flicking down her body. 'Are you here to help me out with that?'

'Well, I'm hardly dressed for it.' But she was talking to air, because he was gone, heading for the doors. He did that a lot.

Hitching her backpack, Gigi took off after him.

'The thing is,' she said, trying to keep up and not draw attention to herself, 'and I know this is completely out of order, and you have every right to tell me to get lost, Mr Kitaev, but we're all really concerned about our jobs. I thought if I could show you a few things you might understand where we're coming from.'

'What exactly have you got to show me?' He didn't break stride.

Well, the flyers and her presentation—but she needed a table for that and he was on the move.

Boy, was he on the move.

'Lots,' she said, mustering all the enthusiasm possible, given the situation. Only to bang straight into his back as he ground to a halt.

She looked up and swallowed. Hard. He was looking down at her in a way that made her want to pull a blanket around herself. A *thick* blanket. Possibly fire retardant.

Oh, boy.

'Tell you what, Red. Can I call you Red?'

Red? Really? 'Okay…sure.'

'You talk; I'll listen—if you can keep up.'

'Keep up with what?' she asked.

'Can you run in those?'

Gigi glanced at her feet, baffled. 'I guess so.'

But when she looked up he was already heading out.

She trailed him onto the pavement, only to watch him power off across the road framed by those two gorillas.

'But I don't *want* to run,' she called after him, even as she began to do just that.

It wasn't easy, with her backpack whacking her on the back like an uncomfortable metronome. The avenue was busy mid-morning. Gigi almost collided with a couple holding hands and her darting sideward leap to avoid disaster landed her in a puddle. Dirty water smeared her jeans.

Apparently he'd meant what he said—and, as much as it made her job harder, she could respect that. People who said what they meant and did what they said could be trusted. She hoped it would translate into a forthright exchange. If she could catch him.

She came close on the corner, just as he turned onto the Avenue des Champs-Élysées.

'Mr Kitaev?' she hollered.

To her relief he slowed his pace.

'Can you keep the shouting out of my name down to a low roar?' he asked as she came alongside him.

'Sure. Sorry.'

'So you're the rebel in the ranks?'

She cast him a worriedly baffled look. 'Not exactly.'

'Yesterday yours was an unusual approach.'

'What approach? I didn't approach you yesterday.'

'The dive from that tank?'

What was he on about? 'I did *not* throw myself off the tank to get your attention.'

'Right...'

'Honestly, I wouldn't endanger my spinal column—I'm not stupid.'

'Horosho.'

Gigi didn't speak a word of Russian, but she got the subtext. He didn't believe her.

Her temper broke like a wave. 'Listen, I don't need to create silly diversions to get a man's attention!'

He thrust a staying arm in front of her as he checked the traffic.

'A word of advice,' he said, scanning the road. 'Don't squeeze your eyes shut. Just let them lie closed naturally, otherwise they twitch. It gave you away.'

What was he talking about now? Irritating man, with his dazzlingly dark brown eyes, the long, thick coal-black lashes sweeping over them above the sharp, deadly planes of his high cheekbones. If you liked that sort of thing...

'I wasn't twitching. *When* was I twitching?'

He meant her fall from the tank. He couldn't possibly think... Good grief, she'd been virtually concussed!

'You were twitching. And ditch the T-shirts while you're

t it,' he said as his arm dropped away and he moved forward. 'Play to your assets.'

'What do you mean, my *assets*?'

He headed across the road.

Gigi's gaze dropped to her chest. He didn't mean what
she thought he meant, did he?

'Hey!' she called, taking off after him. 'I really don't think
you should be saying those kind of things to me!'

Although men had said worse. You had to have a thick
skin in this business. But, really, if he was going to force
her to run through the streets of Paris he could at least be
polite to her! It wasn't easy, even in her trainers. To make
matters worse she had blisters upon blisters on the soles of
her feet, from dancing in brand-new four-inch stilettos last
night. Her feet were killing her!

He should try doing double performances six days a week,
forty weeks of the year for five years—in heels—and see
how he liked being made to run on hard pavement.

She stumbled and narrowly avoided a fire hydrant, and
then dodged around a small dog on a leash.

Stupid Parisians and their dogs...

When she caught up with him she panted, 'I'm just trying to represent the troupe!'

'Why? What do the troupe want?'

Gigi stared at him. The man had barely broken a sweat.
It was so unfair.

'An opportunity—a chance to prove themselves. A pay-
rise!'

She tacked on the last because really, at this point, she
might as well go for gold. She wanted to add, *And not to service you sexually!* But shouting that in the street was further
than she was prepared to go.

She was really hoping she wouldn't have to bring Solange
up—and not just because it was bound to antagonise him.
Frankly, it was embarrassing. But, given he hadn't showed
at the cabaret last night, she couldn't imagine him showing

tonight and wondered how he'd manage to hook up with Solange after all. Not that he'd necessarily ever intended to

It had already crossed her mind that Solange might be lying. It wouldn't be the first time.

A knot in her chest Gigi hadn't known was there loosened a bit.

Not that she'd spent a lot of time thinking about it… She'd just discussed it a little with Lulu last night over crêpes, as they'd walked home up the hill to their flat behind Sacré-Coeur.

The things other girls did to get ahead in the business… The things they would never do… The things they might be prepared to compromise on should they be pushed to the edge…

It had ended in Lulu posing the question, 'So, if your grandma needed a kidney transplant and the *only* way to get it was to sleep with him, would you do it?'

Gigi had pretended to consider it. 'I think I'd have to.'

Lulu had nodded. Then she'd looked at her with those big brown eyes and said solemnly, 'What if she *didn't* need a kidney transplant?'

Which was when they had both dissolved into giggles.

But in the light of day Gigi knew a better question was how would Solange approach this situation?

For one thing, she wouldn't be pounding the pavement after him, blisters bursting in her trainers. Not that Solange had the intelligence to understand that their jobs were at stake. No, all *she* saw was a sexy, famous man and she wanted her piece.

Had she *had* her piece?

Gigi eyed his long broad back, the muscles shifting as he kept up a powerful driving pace. It didn't take much imagination to envisage all that effortless masculine grace and power translating itself into something more intimate, something that required skill and rhythm, something—

Something she shouldn't even be thinking about!

What was wrong with her? His sex life wasn't her business, she told herself sternly, although she was fast losing sight of exactly what *was* her business with him.

Exhaling, she came to a stop. This was useless. He wasn't listening to her. He was amusing himself and she'd turned herself into the punchline of his joke. Nothing new there.

Her shoulders slumped. There didn't seem much point in pursuing this.

Which was when she realised he'd turned back. He moved like some predatory king of the beasts, deceptively at ease as he padded lightly but with a natural authority through the crowds towards her, and the female in her fluttered responsively.

The way he was looking at her as he approached, she could have been the only woman on the street.

Stupid female—she was going to get torn apart if she wasn't careful.

He circled her, forcing her to turn, and turn again, as he looked her up and down.

'What exactly are you going to do for this pay-rise, Red?'

'Dance,' she responded with a little frown.

'Right.' He winked at her and took off again, and she found herself hurrying after him.

This time he kept it to a slow lope, his attention on her. Maybe at last she could get him to listen.

'And when do you take your clothes off?'

'Pardon?' she squeaked.

'That's the bit I'm interested in, Red. I assume I get to see this private dance if I take you back to the hotel?'

Gigi almost hit a traffic sign. She put out her hands to grab the pole.

'What are you talking about?'

'Women throw themselves at me all the time. Why would you be any different?'

'I'm not here for *that*,' she said impatiently, trying to work out what he meant by 'private dance'.

'"That" is sex, and I can get it anywhere. You'll have to up the ante, Red.'

She almost stumbled over her feet. Sex? She wasn't offering him *sex*! Who had said anything about sex?

But he was getting away, and it shot through Gigi, hot and scalding, that this might be the last thing they ever discussed and he was going to go away thinking she was... well, *Solange*!

Her legs stopped working and she just stood there, watching his lean muscular form pound a little further into the distance. Frustrated beyond belief.

'I am *not* here to have sex with you!' she hollered after him.

CHAPTER FIVE

PASSERS-BY ALMOST got whiplash, reacting to her announcement, but Gigi told herself it wasn't that bad. What stank was the fact that this awful, sexist, conceited man thought she had so little respect for herself she'd offer up her body... for what? A pay-rise?

He'd ground to a dangerously ominous halt and now came loping back towards her, his expression enough to send all her 'flee and survive' instincts into overdrive.

'What is this?' he growled.

'I could ask you the same question.' Her voice only shook a little bit. 'Is this how you got your—your grubby hands on L'Oiseau Bleu? By goading Ahmed el Hammoud until he buckled and...and put us in the pot?'

'Interesting turn of phrase.' His gaze narrowed, assessing. 'Know him well, do you, Red?'

Do not rise to the bait, she told herself. *He's doing this to work you up into a frenzy so you'll go away.*

'Even more interesting,' he continued conversationally— as if he *wasn't* crowding her and leaving only a hand span of space between them, as if the hot, hard reality of him *wasn't* pushing her on the back foot. 'Now that I've seen the place I know why it was "in the pot", as you put it. I should have folded.'

'Really?' Her voice came out all high and airless. 'I don't think you'd fold for anyone or anything. I think you like to win, Mr Kitaev, and that means someone has to lose. I don't intend for that to be our fate.'

He was looking at her as if she truly interested him for the first time.

'And what exactly are you going to do, Miss Valente?'

'Fight you.'

Khaled almost smiled.

'Go ahead.' He thought of the people lining up to do just that, half a world away. 'Take your best shot.'

'I will,' she volleyed back. 'Solange Delon!'

She said this as if they were magic words. Clearly it was meant to mean something to him.

'Solange Delon…' she said again, but this time with less confidence, given the lack of a response. 'You asked her to come for drinks. With you. Tonight.'

Nothing.

Gigi could feel the ground shifting under her feet. Somehow she'd got something wrong…

A faint smile began to tug at the firm, sensual line of his mouth.

Gigi's temper quivered. He had no right to smile like that. Not when he didn't even have the decency to own up to it. If there was anything to own up to…

'I just don't think it's right,' she proffered into his continuing silence. 'Picking up a showgirl like one of those plastic Eiffel Towers you buy at a kiosk outside the metro—a souvenir of your trip.'

'Is that what you think, Gigi?' His tone was deceptively soft. 'Or is that what you've read?'

Taken aback, Gigi hesitated.

Well, *everyone* had read it. The marauding Russian, grabbing whatever he could get—cultural artefacts, real estate, women.

She had an odd little visual of him as a cartoonish King Kong, pushing a fistful of showgirls into his open mouth, legs everywhere.

Despite everything, a little part of her wanted to smile.

'I suppose you're going to say it's not true?' she prompted into the tense silence.

He didn't respond.

'To be fair, I guess some of it is exaggeration,' she allowed tightly, knowing she was losing ground fast.

He gave her an unamused half-smile. 'Possibly.'

She reddened.

This wasn't where she'd intended to take things today—she was supposed to be professional.

'Like I said, women throw themselves at me all the time.'

'I guess you can't help being beautiful,' she said grudgingly, then closed her eyes briefly. *Don't tell him he's beautiful, eejit.*

'I was going to say that money has an odd effect on people.' He was watching her as if she fascinated him. 'But if you're going to throw compliments at me, Gigi, you could try aiming at something I might respond to.' His dark Russian accent had a lazy inflection, as if he was enjoying this. 'Most men aren't interested in being told they're beautiful.'

'I'm speaking objectively,' she said stiffly. 'Obviously you're good-looking…'

'Downgraded from beautiful? Keep going.'

She flushed. 'Look, I'm not going to stand here and discuss your looks.'

'You're attracted to me.'

Gigi went rigid. 'I am not! You're nothing like my type.'

'What *is* your type?'

'Sensitive, caring, an animal-lover, good to his mum…' Gigi wasn't sure how they'd got on to this topic, but she did have a list if he wanted to hear it.

'Gay?'

Gigi almost choked. She put her hands on her hips. 'You sound like the stereotype of a homophobic Russian he-man.'

He smiled. 'I'm not homophobic,' he said comfortably, 'and I'm fast revising my opinion of *you*, Red.

'Oh, and what opinion is that?'

'You're not here to have sex with me—you're going to pester me into giving you whatever it is you want.'

Gigi turned pink and told herself she'd rather be a pest than have him think she was trading sexual favours for… well, favours. Only she wasn't making a nuisance of herself, was she?

'You asked me what my type was,' she defended herself. 'And I'm sorry if I'm being a nuisance, but you asked me to run with you!'

'You need a new type.'

He was smiling openly at her now, but instead of feeling irritated she felt her heart pounding in her chest. She wished it would stop—it was most distracting. He should stop smiling too.

He was right. She did need a new type.

But it wasn't going to be him.

Not that he was offering. Apparently she was a pest. Gigi tried not to mind that too much. Besides, gorgeous Russian gazillionaires didn't date jobbing dancers.

Lead dancers at the Lido, maybe. Not chorus girls at L'Oiseau Bleu.

She worried at her lower lip. *Was* she being a pest? There was something so certain and old-fashioned about his masculinity that everything he said had weight to it.

She hadn't had much male certainty in her life. The men she knew were for the most part equivocal and slippery. Witness her dad—and more latterly the Danton brothers, who had effectively stuffed up the only home she'd truly ever had since her mother's death.

Gigi took a breath. Now was not the time to think about what made her want to howl. It was the time to do something about it.

'Look,' she said, instinctively reaching out to touch his arm. 'Let's just forget you said what you said, and you forget I said what I said, and we'll start again.'

Even to her own ears it sounded lame, but right now it was all she had.

He was looking at her hand and she moved to snatch it back, but he caught her fingers between his.

Her eyes jerked up to his, but before she could ask him what he thought he was doing a shower of gravel spattered at their feet, sending Gigi's confused thoughts flying as she followed its source to two boys who were old enough to know better.

A woman who was obviously their mother was on one of the culprits in an instant, clipping him behind the ear as she took hold of the smallest boy's arm none too gently.

'Quittez notre cabaret tout seul!' she said in a tense, tight voice with a sideward glare at Kitaev. *'Barbare!'* she spat.

Leave our cabaret alone! Barbarian!

A young couple had stopped, and the girl pulled out her phone to take a picture.

An older man said, 'Why don't you go back to London, where you belong?'

Gigi would have seen more, but Kitaev had stepped in front of her, effectively blocking her view.

For a moment Gigi was confused. Was he *shielding* her? She stared up at his broad back and felt quite odd, because no man had ever looked to her welfare before, and that it should be this man was, well…confusing.

He didn't even like her.

But she never could stand bullies.

If you can't take the criticism, Gigi, you shouldn't be on the stage.

Fair enough, but her two-faced bully of a father's critiques stayed with her to this day: too freckly, too red, too skinny, too stupid, too much trouble.

She'd learned to blank her expression and keep going. She hadn't had much choice.

Kitaev appeared to be doing the same.

Taking it.

Well, *she* didn't have to.

She scooted around him. 'Hey! Who do you think you are—talking to people you don't even know like that?'

In disbelief Khaled watched Gigi walk up to the woman clutching at the necks of her boys' T-shirts.

'No wonder your children have no manners if this is how *you* behave—and *you*, sir—' she gestured to the older gentleman '—you should get your facts right. He doesn't even live in London! None of you have seen what he's going to do with the cabaret. You're just condemning him out of hand. All of you!'

Given Red's opinion of him, this was interesting.

'Why don't you wait and see before passing judgement? He might just surprise you.'

On the contrary—he would be doing pretty much what they expected. Offloading it to the next buyer, charity or scrapheap. Because he wasn't invested in this heritage crap and this much aggravation wasn't worth the trouble.

'Besides, if people like you would buy a ticket to the show once in a while we wouldn't be in so much trouble in the first place!' Gigi put her hands on her hips, staring them all down.

She should have been funny to watch, and she was, but he also wanted to give her a shake. Why was she bothering? Why was she paying any attention to them? These people's opinions meant nothing. They could and would change with tomorrow's new headlines. Given what he'd said to her, he wasn't even worth her spirited defence.

'Who do you think you are?' demanded the woman accusingly.

It was the moment Gigi didn't know she had been waiting for. She drew herself up to her full five feet eleven inches and opened her mouth...

Khaled said something roughly in Russian.

'That's it,' he said in English. He grabbed her hand. 'Show's over.'

To Gigi's astonishment he began to drag her away.

'Gigi Valente,' she called a little desperately over her shoulder. 'I'm a showgirl at L'Oiseau Bleu. Best cabaret revue in town!'

He jerked her roughly to his side.

'Hey, what are you *doing*?' she snapped at him.

'I could ask you the same thing.'

'I'm trying to promote the cabaret.'

Khaled said a rude word. In English.

He scanned over his shoulder and his features tightened.

Gigi followed his example. People were taking more photographs of them with their phones.

'Do not turn around,' he instructed, 'and do not respond.'

'Fair enough,' Gigi replied, suddenly uncertain as to what was going on, and very aware that they were holding hands.

He glared down at her. 'I cannot *believe* you gave them your name.'

Gigi blinked, her thoughts still on their linked hands. 'Why wouldn't I?' Then the other shoe dropped. 'Oh, crap.'

He eyed her and Gigi frowned. 'What? You think I did it on purpose?'

'Nyet,' he shot back. 'I think you did it the same way you appear to do everything, Gigi—without a firm grasp on the reality of the situation.'

She firmed her mouth. He was referring to her accusations earlier. Accusations she still hadn't apologised for.

Someone else called out, *'Barbare!'*

Gigi shuddered at the viciousness of it. 'What is *wrong* with people?'

'Your cabaret has become a catalyst for public opinion, as you well know, and I'm newsworthy.'

Gigi hadn't been aware that public opinion could be this scary. She yelped as flashes went off in her face and instinctively turned away. Khaled tugged her into the shelter of his body.

'Paparazzi' was the only word she understood in the short volley of Russian invective he released. Although her ability to concentrate was somewhat impaired by being pressed up against him. He was incredibly hard and big and honed, and she was inhaling him like an addict. His scent was the faint spice of aftershave, the musk of his skin and fresh male sweat. It was a heady combination and, given his hand had settled solidly at the base of her spine, she guessed he wanted her to stay where she was.

As suddenly as they'd arrived the photographers were gone, but neither of them shifted.

He was making her very much aware that she was a woman.

'We need to move,' he informed her, his breath brushing her cheek, but he didn't.

Was he feeling it too? Gigi became excessively conscious of the hard muscles of his thighs against hers and how well their bodies fitted together. Warmth began to pool in her loins, her nipples tightened, and all of a sudden she became aware that she wasn't the only one with a problem.

As much as she tried to remind herself that he was a man, and their bodies were smushed together, and it might very well be an involuntary biological function, there was still a part of her that had been hammered by his comment about her being a pest, and her self-confidence staggered to its feet and bloomed a little at this rather impressive confirmation that he wasn't as immune to her as he pretended. *Not so much a nuisance now*, she wanted to say to him.

Which probably shouldn't be a woman's first reaction when she was cosied up in his arms.

She looked up. He was already looking down.

Gigi's breathing quickened. They were so close she could see the golden striations in his dark eyes and something of who he actually *was* as opposed to who she'd imagined him to be. A highly intelligent man who was perhaps insightful enough to see some worth in their cabaret. And perhaps if he recognised that he'd have second thoughts about throwing them to the wolves.

Only the longer they stood there the more uncomfortably aware she was that he could possibly be seeing a little more in her than she would be happy for him—or anyone—to know.

Instinctively she shied away and pulled back.

He unexpectedly took hold of her hand again, curling his fingers around hers. She tried to tug herself free, because it all felt far too intimate, but he had started walking, pulling her along with him.

'What are we doing? What's going on now?'

'We're moving,' he supplied gruffly.

She got that part. Where were they moving *to*?

He produced a mobile phone from his back pocket, thumbed a few buttons and released some Russian to whoever was on the other end.

'Thanks to your big mouth we're both going to be all over the internet,' he shared calmly as he re-pocketed the phone.

'What? What are you talking about?'

But she knew. It sank through her like a stone. She'd stuffed up.

From out of nowhere a group of men swarmed.

Kitaev's arm came around her again. 'It's all right—its Security,' he shared with that same masculine certainty that made her hold on to him as she was hustled in a phalanx towards a smoke-windowed limo that had also come out of nowhere and pulled to the kerb.

Without a word he pushed her forward into the car. She scrambled across the luxury seating, not really being given much choice in the matter.

'I've had some security issues since I arrived in Paris,' he informed her as the car shot forward.

'Issues?' she parroted weakly.

'The usual. Breaches of my privacy, photographers—as you've just seen—approaches from people with axes to grind.'

Gigi pursed her lips and remained silent on that one.

His attention returned to the traffic. 'The truth, if you're interested in it, is that I own some property in the South of France and several companies with holdings in and around Paris. There is no grand plan. L'Oiseau Bleu was an unexpected windfall that has turned into something of a catalyst for all the xenophobic feeling in this city.'

He was watching her broodingly.

'And, for your personal information, Gigi, Solange Delon was publicity. I have a PR team who thought a photograph of me with a French showgirl in full rig and the Danton brothers would put a cap on all the negative publicity doing the rounds.'

And just like that Gigi felt about an inch tall.

'Oh…' she said in a small voice.

He gave her an impatient look. 'Think about it—would I be prowling after showgirls with public opinion being what it is?'

'I guess not.'

The silence between them simmered with the unspoken question—given 'public opinion'—as to why he'd taken her with him on that run and courted the risk of exposure.

'Where are we going?' she voiced, not sure of her footing around him any more.

'My hotel,' he said.

CHAPTER SIX

'I'M SORRY ABOUT all the trouble,' Gigi said awkwardly, struggling out of her seat belt. 'I misjudged everything.'

Yes, she had, Khaled thought, but so had he. The chemistry between them was very strong. It was going to complicate things.

Thankfully the rear entrance to the Plaza Athénée was the scene not of a paparazzi scrum but just a couple of vans making deliveries.

If they were discreet there shouldn't be a problem getting inside and upstairs.

He noticed she was out of the car at lightning speed but slow in approaching the service entrance. She clearly didn't want to go inside.

It raised his ire.

'Keep moving.' He put his hand in the centre of her back and gave her a gentle push forward, because hanging around out here was just inviting trouble.

They were in the middle of the busy lobby when she unexpectedly decided to drop down onto one knee.

He almost tripped over her.

'What the hell are you doing?'

She pushed back her unruly fringe and looked up a bit furtively. 'Don't worry about me—you go on, I'll find my own way home.'

Frustration warred with something else. He ignored the something else and very nearly hauled her to her feet—only they were once more in public, and he'd had enough scenes with this woman to sell tickets.

Mademoiselle Valente was going to sit down in the reception room of his suite while he dealt with this via telephone to his lawyer and Jacques Danton. He frowned down at her—only to encounter her behind as she crouched over, delineated in skin-tight denim like a perfect peach. His thoughts simmered... *Da*, either a phone call or he'd peel down those jeans and have her up against that wall over there. Whichever came first.

His attention slid from her peachy bottom to what it was holding them up—only to discover she had one heel wedged out of her trainer and appeared to be... Was she bleeding?

To Gigi's complete astonishment her new boss hunkered down beside her and had her laces loosened before she could react.

'Um...what are you doing?'

Although it was pretty clear what he was doing. He was lifting her left foot in his big capable hands and attempting to slide her shoe off.

She hissed at the dragging contact, and then realised he'd have her sock off in a moment.

He'd have her sock off!

'Hey—no, stop that!' She toppled back onto her backside and scuttled across the marble floor, one shoe on, one shoe off, aware that she was attracting attention, which was something neither of them wanted at this point, but he couldn't hang that one on her. *He* was the guy with the foot fetish!

He eyed her with a mixture of amusement and exasperation. 'I'm not attacking you, *zhenshchina*.'

'I didn't say you were.' She eyed him warily.

He stood up, all shoulders and amused appraisal as he looked her over.

'Just you stay there, and I'll stay here, and we'll keep our hands and feet to ourselves,' she said hastily.

There was no way she was showing this beautiful god of a man her *feet*!

No one saw her feet. Not even Lulu.

Other hotel patrons were stopping to stare at the one-shoed girl on the floor.

Gigi could feel heat creeping into her cheeks.

She tried to shove her foot back into her shoe, but it

had swelled up and it was like trying to shoehorn a balloon in there.

Giving up, she clambered to her feet, trainer in hand.

People were looking. Well, let them look.

She turned in the other direction and had limped a few paces to the doors when a big hand closed around her elbow and his breath brushed her ear.

'The lifts are this way, *kotyonok*.'

Confused, Gigi shivered at the unfamiliar word and the intimate contact.

He turned her in the direction of the lifts.

'The exit is over there,' she protested, not sure why he was prolonging the agony or why she didn't dig her heels in. Other than the fact that they hurt and two hundred plus pounds of arrogance and muscle was steering her into the lift. She gave it one last try. 'Mr Kitaev, I don't think this is such a hot idea.'

'Probably not—and we've established its Khaled.'

His hand slipped from her elbow to the small of her back and rested there, and she stopped struggling.

'Are those photos really going to end up on the internet?' she asked in a strangled voice as the lift doors closed.

'Undoubtedly.'

Gigi noticed he hadn't removed his hand from her back. She moistened her lower lip and tried to conjure up the will to tell him to take his hands off her. Her will was weak.

'Those pictures…will people put derogatory captions to them?'

'Possibly.'

She tried not to sag visibly.

'Could you ring me or something and let me know when they are up? I can give you my number.' *Subtle, Gisele.* She moistened her lips. 'Or I guess you could contact me at the cabaret,' she added awkwardly, wondering if he thought offering up her number smacked of a bit too much intimacy.

His hand shifted lightly on her back to curl around her waist.

Okay, maybe not. Intimacy apparently wasn't a problem...

'What time is tonight's performance?' he asked.

'Hmm?' Gigi wrenched her mind away from his hand on her waist. 'Eight o'clock.' Was he going to turn up? Her spirits lifted. She looked up at his ridiculously masculine profile. Had she actually got through to him?

'By the time you go onstage, Gigi, everyone in Paris will have seen them.'

Her hopes plummeted. 'Oh...'

'Precisely.'

The doors slid open and she waited, not sure what they were doing here. Khaled slid the rest of his arm around her waist and the other beneath her, lifting her effortlessly into his arms.

She was forced to grapple with his big, incredibly solid shoulders and hang on.

'What are you doing?' she thought she should ask.

'Looking after you.'

Gigi's mouth opened and shut. She was, after all, twenty-five years old and had been looking after herself for the past several years with some success. Still, she'd never actually been carried in a man's arms before, and like most women she'd harboured a bit of a fantasy about it...

He was moving, forcing her to hook her arms a bit more securely around his neck, effectively plastering her breasts to his chest. Gigi told herself it was purely a matter of necessity.

'You really don't have to do this,' she felt obliged to say.

'I am aware of that.'

He opened glass doors into the entrance room to his suite and luxury wrapped around them.

'Nice,' she said inadequately.

This earned her a brief, 'Not my taste.'

'Why are you staying here, then?'

'I needed an entire floor over the weekend for security reasons and this hotel provided that.'

He carried her through a very luxurious living area, down a hall and into a bedroom. It contained a very big bed.

Gigi wondered for the first time if she oughtn't to tell him he shouldn't confuse her with Solange?

Not that there had ever *been* anything with Solange…according to him. She was reserving judgement on that.

But still, she didn't bounce on beds with men she'd only just met.

'You could fit ten people on that mattress,' she pointed out in a high, airless voice not quite her own.

He didn't respond.

'I'm just imagining the troupe all laid out like sardines in a can,' she felt obliged to explain.

He looked at her as if she'd said something ridiculous, but she told herself he wasn't a woman in a man's hotel room, being carried around like luggage.

Maybe she should make it clear. 'I'm just saying…don't get any ideas.'

'About these other girls?'

Gigi bit her lip. She wanted to say, *About me*, but clearly he wasn't having any ideas. She was the one entertaining a fantasy.

'I'm just saying,' she mumbled, embarrassed. 'Anyway, in practice it wouldn't work. There'd be fights.'

He gave a gruff snort.

Gigi craned her head over his shoulder but, nope, he showed no interest in the bed. He didn't even break stride.

He definitely hadn't confused her with Solange.

He dumped her on the bathroom vanity.

Gigi was greeted with her reflection, which drove any thoughts of being confused with sexy girls who dated movie stars out of her head. She looked *awful*.

All of her freckles had become heat blotches and swarmed together like angry little ants at a picnic.

He looked—well, hot and sexy. Although all that brooding intensity and muscled capability was currently being channelled into running a tap.

Which was odd.

A sudden unreasoning panic gripped her. Had he brought her back here to punish her for the photographers? Was this some kind of set-up? If he wasn't bent on seduction why else would he bring her up here?

He took hold of her feet.

'Wow. Okay—stop there.' She clamped her hands over his, eyeing him warily. 'I'll deal with the wear and tear. There's nothing to see here.'

'What's the problem?' His dark eyes flickered over her face. 'I doubt you've got anything I haven't seen before.'

Had he just glanced at her chest when he said that?

Gigi felt her nipples tingle inside the soft cups of her sweater girl bra.

Uh-oh. This was *not* good.

Her relationships with men thus far had been of the duck and weave variety. As far as Khaled was concerned she was pretty much a sitting duck.

She was so distracted by her thoughts that she didn't immediately catch him working her socks off. As her cracked heels appeared she yelped, dragged back her feet like pulling up a drawbridge and wedged herself in hard against the mirror.

He said something in Russian and looked her up and down, as if she were a problem he had to solve.

But she didn't care. If there was anything seriously unsexy about her it was her feet. It was where all the damage and scarring almost twenty years of dance had wrought was so violently on display. It was like a confession. Nothing had been easy and she had paid a price, and right now she wasn't confessing to *him*!

'What is the problem now?'

His Russian accent was heavier, and that just upped the sexy quotient—which wasn't helping.

And what did he mean *now*? As if she'd been causing problems left right and centre...? He was a fully paid-up member of their trouble brigade. She wasn't wearing total responsibility for the disasters of this morning.

'There is no problem,' she grumbled. 'I just want to look after this myself.'

He looked sceptical.

'I didn't ask to be brought up here, you know. I didn't ask for all this attention.'

He gave her a long, searching look that implied she had. Which was so unfair!

Gigi wriggled uncomfortably. His gaze dropped lower and caught on something.

What now? Gigi looked down. She'd been aware that her midriff was bare, her T-shirt having worked its way up in all the manhandling, but she hadn't given any thought to the fact that because her jeans were low-riders she was showing off quite a lot of skin—nor to the fact that the indent of her belly button rose high above them, exposing her piercing.

Before she could even think to pull her T-shirt down he brushed his knuckles over her navel and set the miniature silver bell tinkling.

'It's a bell,' she said. Cringed. Could she sound more stupid?

He did it again, his touch unbearably gentle. Suggestive of how he would be in another even more intimate situation.

Gigi bit her lip.

Lifted her eyes to his.

He was smiling at her. 'I wondered what that sound was.' His accent had thickened.

Her breathing grew rapid and shallow in response.

She was now throbbing ever so subtly between her legs. All he had to do was touch her again for a little longer and that throbbing was going to detonate.

The problem was it also drew her attention to the way she was angled against him, thighs apart, virtually inviting him into heaven.

She could hear Lulu's lecture: *'There are really only two situations in a woman's life when she should be displayed at this angle to a man, and if that man isn't her significant other he should be her gynaecologist.'*

Denim or no, Gigi felt self-conscious, and she brought her knees down fast—only now he was standing between them and she was stuck…unless he moved.

He moved. Almost nonchalantly, but she wasn't fooled. And with the flats of his hands on the bench on either side of her she was trapped.

This was his move. He was making a move on her.

Gigi's heart began to flutter like crazy, because he was so close, and he smelt so good, and the energy pulsing between them was like jungle drums in her blood.

She swallowed, unable to break the clasp of his gaze.

Sweet heaven, she had to find a way off this bench. Because so much more than a full reveal of her manky feet was barrelling towards them, and she really didn't want to be the showgirl who gave it up on a bathroom vanity to the man who might or might not be instrumental in taking away the livelihoods of the Bluebirds.

And—oh, God—he was *smiling* at her.

'So what's the problem with your feet?'

This time his dark drawl sounded a lot less impatient, as if whatever the problem was he'd be willing to take the time to fix it.

Immediately her mind went to her other problem and how much time he might devote to *that*…

She cleared her strangled throat. 'There's no problem.'

He vibrated the bell with the tip of his thumb and she made a soft, inarticulate sound. He raised his knowing eyes to hers. The air between them pulled taut.

'Tinker Bell,' he said.

'Tinker Bell?' she echoed doubtfully.

'I read the book when I was a boy and I always had a thing for Tink—little nuisance that she was. Wendy didn't do it for me.'

Gigi narrowed her blue eyes at him and he wanted to laugh, because telling a woman she reminded you of a fairy from an old children's book was almost as crazy as what he was doing right now—sliding the pads of his middle and forefinger over the incredibly silken flesh just below her navel, stroking her there.

He only needed to slide his fingers a couple of inches south and he could snap the buttons on her jeans. Another couple of inches and he'd know exactly what she was wearing under the denim. Another couple and sweet, perfect nirvana.

'Stop that,' she croaked, nipping at her lower lip.

He drew back his hand into a tight fist and exhaled roughly.

She was right.

He exhaled. 'So what about these feet?'

Her mouth dropped open slightly but he had already slid his hands under her soles and brought them up onto the bench.

She didn't fight him this time, but drew up her knees, eyes squeezed shut, like a woman about to endure a root canal at the dentist. It would have been funny had he not been so deeply, unambiguously aroused. So hard it hurt.

He deftly and carefully eased off her socks and tossed them into the wastepaper basket, never to be heard from again. It was a hard shove to his unambiguous impulse to bury himself in her soft, agile beauty to discover how torn up her feet were. He thoughtfully stroked his thumb along the welts criss-crossing the top of her feet. This damage seemed to be from long ago, the scars faded to white.

She had narrow, knobby-toed feet, shaped by the years she'd used them to sculpt the exquisitely formed female body sitting before him. The raised white welts, however, didn't make a lot of sense.

When he was a boy, living in the mountains, he'd learned to fix the wings of birds and splint broken legs for all kinds of small mammals. His stepfather had patiently taught him, along with lessons in how to track and perform a clean kill. Before everything had gone wrong. Before he'd understood that with every year he grew more and more like his father in both feature and reputation.

And being bullied from the age of eight had nothing to do with him being good with his fists and quick to take offence.

He rubbed the pads of his thumbs over her calluses and she made a sound of despair.

He understood shame. He understood what it could do to you if you didn't fight it.

'Relax,' he said, looking up, but her eyes were squeezed shut again, as if that way she could hide.

Her very real dismay loosened the loop of memory that had momentarily tethered him to the past and the tightness in him lifted. Something softer fought for room. He knew how to make her forget her shame, her fear.

He took one of her long, narrow feet in his hands and pressed his thumbs into the sensitive cord of muscle where her foot arched. Avoiding her broken blisters, he dragged his thumbs along the soles of her feet.

She moaned, and her blue eyes shot wide to meet his in honest bewilderment.

A deep satisfaction stirred within him.

He knew how to handle her. Because under her shock, like a promise, was a sensuality as natural and unadorned as she was.

She was a beautiful wild thing he had caught, and he could see a pulse hammering at the base of her throat. But he knew how to handle a frightened wild creature...

CHAPTER SEVEN

'Good?'

'Don't…' she groaned. When clearly she meant *more*.

He pushed again.

She gave a helpless moan and gave herself up to the relief. He kept working until the tension lifted off her and her head rolled back and she moaned again—a deep, utterly unself-conscious sound. Incredibly sexy. He felt it deep in his groin.

'Good?'

She made another approving sound.

Too good. He was dangerously close to losing control himself.

'This might hurt.'

Gigi hissed like a kettle as he slid her feet into the water.

Tender, exposed new skin didn't mix with water—even Plaza Athénée water.

Gigi cracked open one eye and then the other.

She hadn't been able to look at him while he worked on her ugly feet, and now she scanned his face anxiously for signs of disgust. Only she could find none.

He made quick work of the caked blood with the dexterous use of a flannel, before letting out the water and wrapping her feet in the sleek hand towel folded beside the basin.

His practicality saved her from real embarrassment.

'Thank you,' she said, a little at a loss as to what else to say.

She wasn't used to being looked after, she realised, and that it should be by this tough, intimidating man confused her.

He had handled her feet with a care and generosity that had once again made her mind wander to what else he could do with those large hands… She eyed him almost shyly.

'You're a funny girl' was all he said.

Gigi's warm feelings faded.

She'd heard that before. 'Gigi the Clown'. Her papa's fail
safe response to her falls, tumbles and general efforts to ge
him to pay attention to her.

'Funny ha-ha, or funny crazy?' she asked, her voice a
little raw.

He glanced up at her, as if she'd said something odd, hi
dark eyes making her tummy flip.

'Funny sexy.' he said, as if it was obvious, and she be
lieved him. He set the towel aside.

Sexy? Offstage sexy? Really?

He opened what was clearly a first aid kit and took ou
cotton wool, antiseptic and plasters.

She bit her lip. 'They're not pretty,' she said in a low voice

She *hated* this—hated it that she felt obliged to point i
out, hated laying herself bare. She'd rather just strip off al
her clothes and distract him with what she knew worked fo
an audience of seven hundred every night.

'You're a dancer. You've got a dancer's feet.'

'I know, but the other girls don't have half my damage.'

He raised his eyes to hers and she saw a lot of questions
most of which Gigi really didn't want to answer. But at the
same time she didn't want to make them too much of a big
deal.

'When I was in my early teens I was in a highwire act
and it involved twisting cords around my feet. My papa said
the scarring would go away, but it never did.'

'Your father? How was he involved?'

'He managed the circus—Valente's International.' She
couldn't help lifting her chin a little. In spite of everything
she remained proud of that heritage. 'Valente's had been a
family concern for almost a hundred years when my father
was bankrupted.'

'You were an acrobat?'

'Not a very good one,' she admitted. 'But it cured me of
any residual fear of heights.'

Being driven up a rope with your father yelling that you were holding up rehearsal had effectively removed that fear.

'This is criminal,' he said, running his thumb over a welt. 'What kind of a father allows this to happen to his daughter?'

Her heart was pounding. His questions were grazing too close to some painful truths in her past.

'That's not for you to judge,' she answered stiffly. 'You weren't there. It's a hard life—you have to be seasoned to perform every night. The pain is a part of it.' She could hear her father's voice, lecturing her on this.

'Yet you're ashamed?'

Gigi hesitated. 'I—'

'You have nothing to be ashamed of, Red.'

'I know that,' she said quickly.

She stared at her feet, wondering why she was even telling him all this. 'Do you think you could stop calling me Red?' She looked up. 'I'm Gigi...or Gisele—'

'Gisele.'

Gigi's breath caught at the way his dark Russian accent turned her name into something quite beguiling.

Feminine.

'It's beautiful.'

His sincerity was a lot to take in. She blinked. Looked down and flexed her toes. 'Unlike my feet.'

He looked at her seriously for a moment from those dark assessing eyes, and then straightened and whisked his T-shirt up and off.

Gigi was almost blinded by all that gorgeous golden skin suddenly on display, pulled taut over slabs of muscle and not an ounce of fat that she could see.

His physique wasn't fine and lightweight, like the boys she danced with. Although lean, it was heavy with broad bones and muscle, his chest covered in fine dark hair. Gigi's fingers stirred restlessly with the urge to tangle her fingers in it.

He was most definitely a different breed from the men she was used to. It wasn't quite fanciful to say looking at him half stripped was like being introduced to the male sex for the first time.

'Take a look at this,' he said, in that deep gruff voice.

He presented her with his gloriously defined back, reaching up to place his fingertips above a nasty scar on his left shoulder. 'This one was caused by a bullet—it lodged in bone, shattered my scapula—and here...' He took her much smaller hand and put it on his lean waist, where something had left a seven-inch incision that had healed badly and left a raised white scar. 'Knife wound.'

He turned around.

'The discolouration here...' He pulled his waistband away from the line of his lean muscled hip, revealing a taut pelvic cradle and dark hair arrowing down to his sex and a splash of darker pigmentation where some of the skin, obviously puckered, indicated burns. He spoke calmly but in a low voice. 'That was an explosion on a road that was supposed to have been cleared.'

Gigi stroked her fingers over the old wound, viscerally aware that she was touching his bare flesh and that he felt hot and hard and male. But on a more conscious level she was horrified by the kind of life he'd led to cause these injuries. The raised skin she had under her fingertips was testimony to the poor medical care he'd received. Bullets? Knives?

'How did you get these?'

'National Service. Hunting.'

He was looking down at her now with a faint smile, the nature of which would have made a more virtuous girl uneasy. Although Gigi guessed she *was* that virtuous girl.

'I've got more, but that would involve removing more clothing than you're probably comfortable with.'

Gigi had opened her mouth to tell him she felt pretty comfortable with clothing being removed when she caught the glint in his eyes.

Her breath caught.

He wanted her.

Before she could properly react his arm was going around her, his hand was at the back of her head, delving gently into her hair, and she only had a moment to look into his eyes before he lowered his mouth to hers.

He just *took* that kiss.

The confidence of his move left her with nowhere to go, and Gigi found herself going under with the sensuous slide of his mouth over hers. She parted her lips, the masculine taste of him invading every pore of her being. Her lashes drifted down. He didn't hurry it—he *enjoyed* it.

She clutched at him, giving way to his superior technique. No one had ever kissed her like this before. It was ravishing, and she never wanted him to stop.

But he did.

He released her after just one kiss, leaving her stunned and slightly panting.

'This is bad idea,' he said thickly in broken English, his fingers still sifting the soft hair at the nape of her neck, still staring at her mouth.

She didn't want it to be a bad idea—she didn't want him to stop. She *ached*.

She really wanted another kiss.

She was going to get one.

Gigi slapped her hand to his chest and spread her fingers like a starfish, using his chest hair to tug him back in the direction she wanted him.

'I don't think so,' she said, looking determinedly into his dark eyes.

Something clean and wild pierced through the guard she had become used to seeing in his eyes, as if everything else had been a cover for what lived inside him and she'd just woken it up.

Gigi had a flashback to that moment at the cabaret when

he'd turned around and she'd imagined he was going to devour her.

She just hadn't thought it would be literally.

A primitive thrill unlike any she'd ever known zinged
along her spine to her brain, knocking out all the realities
of their situation.

The paparazzi…who he was…who she was…the cabaret. Gone.

They were just a man and a woman.

Their mouths met, his fused hungrily to hers once more,
and the scrape of his tongue was tasting her, his hand holding
the back of her head the better to angle the kiss. It wasn't polite or gentle or coaxing. It was rough and raw and it sparked
spot fires in her body Gigi couldn't reach to put out.

Instinctively she wrapped her arms around his neck and
there was a clatter as the first aid gear went flying. She was
caught by her legs and she clamped them around his lean,
hard waist.

He swung her off the vanity, big hands cupping her behind, and with their mouths still fused he strode from the
bathroom, carrying her with him.

It was all happening so fast, and Gigi wasn't sure why
but she just knew that if they slowed down one of them
would stop this.

He was stripping back her jacket and she was helping
him, using her steely thigh muscles like grips to hold onto
him. She wasn't sure what she really wanted here, but he'd
freed something in her that had been caught, that she'd never
known until now, and she felt a little wild with it.

Her breasts sang with sensation, squashed up against his
chest as she fought free of her jacket.

Under the press of her pelvis he was formidably aroused,
and it was a shot to her ego that she could do this to him.
Then she was free to hold him tightly to her and kiss him
back, a little drunk on the taste, aware that this was so out
of character nobody who knew her would recognise her.

His knees hit the side of the bed and he lowered her on to her back in an economical move that spoke of much practice.

But not practice with L'Oiseau Bleu showgirls, and that was what counted.

He was pushing up her T-shirt, cupping her breasts, lifting himself so he could see her.

Her common sense was shouting. *This is not going to fix the cabaret. This is only going to get you into trouble.*

But still she ran her hands up his chest, revelling in his solidity and strength, looping her arms around his neck before he could get her bra off. She dragged his mouth down to hers again. His beard wasn't scratchy at all. It was soft. It felt delicious.

Her hands went shyly to his waistband, because she'd never been a girl to waste time, which was when she felt resistance shoot through his body. In the same instant his hand snapped like a handcuff around her wrist.

'No, you don't.'

His gruff words hit her like a bucket of cold water.

He released her wrist and what she saw in his dark eyes told her he was calling a halt to this—something *she* should have done minutes ago.

That he could pull back now, when she was still hot and bothered and clinging to him, was just horribly embarrassing.

As he moved away from her Gigi knew she should be getting upright fast, playing it just as cool and together as he appeared to be.

Only she discovered she wasn't that sophisticated. Or maybe it was that it had been so long since she'd been in a situation like this. With an actual. Live. Man.

Holy moly—when had she *ever* been in a situation like this?

He's your boss.

He was also a million years beyond her in sophistication, and she was proving that right now by squeezing her eyes shut, as if he might disappear, and she would wake in her own room, and all of this would be just one of those embarrassing being-caught-in-public-naked dreams.

When she found the wherewithal to crank up an eyelid she discovered he was standing over her, running his hands through his hair where only moments before her fingers had been. He was looking rueful, and because of it younger—more his twenty-nine years than the über-successful man of the world she'd spent the last hour or so with.

An hour, Gigi, and you're flat on your back on his bed?

She watched his biceps flex as he massaged the back of his neck and was distracted for a moment—until she realised what she was doing. She was acting like a sex-crazed rabbit!

'This isn't wise.'

His voice was rough and deep, and crushingly certain as his gaze ran over her, rumpled and prone and probably unattractively flushed, still lying on the bed.

No? Gigi struggled to prop herself up on her elbows.

She wondered what he meant to do. Was she supposed to say something?

'I need a shower.'

Did he?

She watched him go, uncertain of the etiquette. Still a little dazed and confused. What had she done wrong?

Not what—who, you eejit. You're a Bluebird, and he's the boss, and this is not what you came for.

She looked down at her breasts, which had been so happy beneath his hands, and at her nipples, which were still standing up like two little soldiers on parade.

Not today, ladies.

She watched the door close and she was left on her own in the middle of the glamorous bed. Her squeak firmly in place.

Khaled stepped out of the shower, his body under control after the effects of chill-level water, aware that this brief taste of Gigi had made her even more dangerous.

He knew now how she felt—soft, pliant, wild. How she

moved her mouth—sensuously. How she used her tongue, and the little sounds she made that were enough to tip him over the edge.

She was the sweetest, wildest thing.

He blew out a deep breath. Only not for him.

He'd caught himself a Bluebird—but with photographs of them together on the internet there was no way he could do what would clearly come far too naturally for both of them, it appeared.

It would not be conducive to a quick sale of the cabaret.

For now, he had to get her out of here.

He stepped into the bedroom and found—nothing.

The only sign of what had occurred was the rumpled coverlet and the scent of her—something like cinnamon and sugar baked hot. It made his mouth water.

'Gigi?'

Silence.

He'd dropped her backpack on the seat at the end of the bed and it was gone too.

Khaled stood with his hands resting lightly on his lean towel-wrapped hips and wondered at the disappointment dropping through him. He'd misjudged her. How in hell had he misjudged her? He'd been so wide of the mark he needed either a psychologist, to find out where his native intelligence had gone, or a sex therapist to work out at exactly what point what was between his legs had superseded his brain.

Thumping something suddenly appealed.

All that sweet, eccentric confusion she trailed—like breadcrumbs to the doorstep of that cabaret of hers. A con. How had he missed it?

He should have been analysing that the moment her thighs had locked decisively around his hips and her breasts, like the plump little weapons of male destruction they were, had hit his chest—not being concerned about her well-being and whether he was pushing this too quickly, and exactly how fast was too fast to peel her jeans off.

Yanking on his own pair of jeans and fighting into a fresh shirt, he wondered at his own credulity.

He'd been on the receiving end of women looking for a pay-off too many times to be this careless.

The problem was it had been her obvious distress and confusion when the paps had descended which had muddied his reactions.

She didn't act like a woman on the make—she came across instead as a lively, extroverted girl who incidentally had a cabaret to promote, and in the next breath as a vulnerable young woman with a past that sounded at best colourful and at worst abusive, given he'd seen her feet.

It had been instinct that had had him tugging off his T-shirt and showing her his own scars, wanting to take the sting out of her embarrassment about her own. He hadn't counted on how good her hands had felt on his body, and for a few minutes there she'd been utterly happy to accommodate him on the bathroom vanity. Seemingly *gratis*. No emotional fallout or extended lines of communication required.

It was a scenario that didn't happen in his life any more. Not since he'd made his first million. There was always a catch.

What he had discovered now wasn't unfamiliar, but somehow he'd let down his guard with her, and oddly her departure felt like a kick to the guts.

He snorted.

Focus, man.

She hadn't got what she wanted and she was gone—simple. Now he needed to make an overdue call to his personal legal advisor and find out what he could do about those photos.

CHAPTER EIGHT

KHALED HAD HIS phone out as he wandered barefoot into the main living room, with its explosion of taffetas and velvets, but he never made that call.

Sitting on the sofa, with her impossibly long legs curled under her, her coppery head bent as she worked, was Gigi.

With a laptop.

He moved up silently behind her. A part of him was asking what the hell he was doing. What had he expected? To find her uploading photos of his hotel room? Possibly. Privacy was something nobody could take for granted any more.

He stopped behind the sofa. The screen in front of her was full of images of L'Oiseau Bleu.

'Gigi?'

She almost jumped off the sofa. 'Oh, Mary and Joseph, you scared me.'

After an initial moment of eye contact she guiltily returned her attention to the screen almost immediately.

His instincts prowled. He glanced at the screen—more in an attempt to work her out than out of any real interest in what she was doing. 'What is this?' he asked, more abruptly than he'd meant to.

'I'm just gathering some things I want to show you about the cabaret's history…its importance to Paris. I thought seeing as I'm up here…' Her voice ran away and she clicked on another image—one of the cabaret in its heyday.

Khaled was more interested in the laptop. Had she run with *that* in her backpack?

Come to think of it, the thing hadn't been light when he'd been carrying it around.

'Maybe this is a bad idea,' she said, still intent on avoiding eye contact. 'You probably don't have time to take a look. I should probably get out of your hair.'

She was putting down the lid on the laptop and unfolding her long legs.

He moved fast and dropped down onto the sofa beside her, reached for it.

'Show me what you've got.'

He'd jumped her in the bathroom—he could give her five minutes.

What she had was clusters of images, reviews, articles, all informatively cascading one after the other.

'This is our current show—we've been performing it for the last three years.'

The screen was filled with colour and movement and cheesy eighties dance music.

He was about to tell her she could skip this part when he zeroed in on Gigi, descending the stairs with a line of other showgirls.

She looked like a glittering peacock, dragging a shimmering tail. Her arms were gracefully outstretched, an elaborate neck-piece of glittering rhinestones falling from her throat to cover her chest, but doing nothing to hide the fact that all the girls who weren't wearing rhinestone bras were topless.

The warmth of Gigi's very real body beside him and the memory of the very real breasts he'd had his hands on was making a mockery of his decision to keep his hands off her.

One act succeeded the next—primarily *tableaux vivants* that involved the girls wearing as little as possible. In between there was a chanteuse, a performing dog, a barbershop quartet and some magic tricks. It was certainly different.

He folded his arms, switched off the male part of his brain that kept fixating on her breasts, and allowed himself to appreciate the very real charm of it.

Eventually she hit 'stop' and looked at him expectantly.

Until now he hadn't been convinced that it was anything more than a glorified strip joint. Frankly, he wasn't sure *what* it was. On the one hand there was all the charm and femininity of the over-the-top dance numbers. Even the male dancers looked as if they'd been neutered. On the other hand there were the boobs and the bottoms that gave it its risqué reputation. But that was very French. Gigi had been telling him the truth, and now he understood a little of why Paris was going slightly bonkers over the idea of him laying a hand on their precious L'Oiseau Bleu.

She was good. He hadn't expected her to be this good.

'What do you think?'

He thought that he was hard and aching, and it had nothing to do with what he'd just seen on this screen and everything to do with the sweet sexiness of the girl curled up beside him, who at every turn had proved herself to be not quite what he'd thought she was.

He looked into her hopeful, obviously secretly pleased expression and began to wonder exactly what was going on in that eccentric little head of hers.

Gigi congratulated herself on the professional way she was conducting herself. She'd kept her hands to herself and she was almost the whole way through her presentation. Really, nobody could find fault.

If you put aside the bodyguard incident in the lobby. The incident with the crowd on the Champs-Élysées. The incident with the paparazzi. The incident in the lobby with her shoes and—she closed her eyes briefly—the incident on the bathroom vanity, ending with her flat on her back in the bedroom, about which the less she thought the better.

No, all in all, putting those things aside, she'd handled this quite well.

Somehow she'd come through it all and had him where she'd wanted him hours ago, before all this began.

On a sofa, glued to her presentation.

It was time to fire some questions at him.

But first of all she made herself look him in the eye— the first time she'd done so since he'd sat down beside her.

After all, she wasn't ashamed of her perfectly healthy

sex drive. And she guessed she would have remembered soon after he did that this was a professional relationship and called a halt.

Only lifting her gaze to those velvet-lashed dark eyes she was instantly out of her depth again, and she knew to her embarrassment that whatever hadn't happened between them was all down to him.

She'd been the one kicking things and climbing over the poor man and forcing him to stroke her breasts.

'So what do you think?' she asked in a strangled voice.

'Impressive.'

Impressive? Really? She caught herself in time. *He doesn't mean your breasts, Gigi!*

Although, actually, stroking her breasts had been down to him…

Stop thinking about your breasts!

She cleared her throat. 'I was wondering if you'd given any thought to what road you might go down,' she ventured. 'We'd like to stay family-friendly.'

'Family-friendly?'

Gigi's optimism dwindled a little. Why did he have to say it as if it was a concept he wasn't entirely familiar with?

'We're sexy, but you can bring your mum. Family-friendly,' she explained. 'I mean obviously we'd have to keep our "Sixteen and Over" door rule…'

'Obviously.'

She resisted looking up at his dry tone, pretending instead to be interested in sorting through a few images of the current show as she wondered exactly how far she could push this without blurting out, *We don't want to become a nasty men's club.*

'It's a concern, given your other…um…holdings.'

'I own gambling venues, some nightclubs, hotels…'

She glanced up.

'No strip joints, Gigi,' he said with a faint smile.

She moistened her lips. 'It's just that when the girls took

off their pasties and started writhing unimaginatively round poles burlesque died.'

Khaled tried to imagine Gigi arching against a pole in nothing much. Curiously, it wasn't a salacious image. Instead it was one that made him feel like the morals police. In his mind he barricaded the stage and put up 'Nothing To See Here' signs, wrapped her in a robe and hustled her towards the exit.

He cleared his throat. 'Pasties?'

'Nipple shields—tassels sometimes.'

He frowned.

She gave a sigh, as if he were being deliberately obtuse, and spelt it out. 'Tit tape.'

'Does this mean you're not actually topless?'

He was speaking generally, but he suddenly wanted to know specifics. Specifically Gigi, and exactly how much of her was on show.

He'd seen a screen full of topless showgirls swathed in ropes of rhinestones falling from elaborate neck-pieces, nipples peeking through. It wasn't exactly salacious—you could see just as much flesh on most beaches in Europe—but he was a man…he knew how other men would be looking at it.

He'd got the distinct impression those were her nipples he was seeing on that screen. It took a manful effort not to let his gaze drift down to her chest, given that the real thing had been under his hands not long ago, and the memory of her nipples poking enthusiastically into his palms wasn't going away.

More blood rushed to his groin.

No, that wasn't going away either.

'Bare breasts are a traditional part of French cabaret,' Gigi said, looking blameless as sunlight. 'But a cabaret is not a strip joint. The emphasis in French cabaret is on fun, humour and glamour. There's no sleaze.'

'The entertainment division of the Kitaev Group is principally gaming and music venues.' He watched her teeth sink into the lush promise of her lower lip and found his voice had thickened again when he added, 'No poles.'

Gigi wasn't too sure if she believed him. Oh, she believed him about the poles, but his plan for L'Oiseau Bleu was another thing.

Gaming and music venues?

Don't frown, she told herself.

'You don't look too happy about that, Gigi.'

She understood that he was humouring her, but she took his question seriously all the same. 'I'm just concerned, given you own some pretty outlandish venues.'

He gave her a smile. 'I admit the Oasis Pearl in Dubai is fairly over the top, but it has to be to compete.'

Gigi made a mental note to look up the Oasis Pearl on the internet.

'And what would make L'Oiseau Bleu...*compete*?' She tested out the word and tried to sound as if she knew of what she spoke.

'Why don't you tell me?'

Drat.

'I'm not really a businesswoman,' she mumbled, 'I'm a dancer.'

'Why did you come to me, Gigi?'

It was a good question, and one she'd asked herself many times over since she'd discovered L'Oiseau Bleu had passed into new hands.

'I guess it's because the other girls needed a spokesperson and I kind of elected myself.' She met his eyes. 'And, unlike them, I know what L'Oiseau Bleu once was, and I have an idea of what it could be again. With the right person at the helm.'

There it was. The sincerity. Khaled couldn't deny that she appeared to believe what she said. It went against his grain to lie to her, but after her little performance on the Champs-Élysées he couldn't risk handing over the sensitive information that he was passing on the cabaret only to see it broadcast the length and breadth of Paris before nightfall.

Gigi had a mouth on her. She'd proved it.

He couldn't risk telling her the truth.

'The other girls are loyal to the theatre,' she said quickly, as if wanting to disabuse him of the notion she was a one-woman crusade, 'but I don't think they really understand how far downhill the cabaret has gone in the past few decades...' She trailed off. 'Sorry, I get carried away. You don't have to do anything. I mean, you could sell us on. It's not as if we saw anything of the last owner.'

'Ahmed el Hammoud?'

'We never met him. Do you know him?'

'I know he's useless at cards.' The oil sheikh's incompetence at poker meant Khaled now possessed some nice Arabian breeding stock and a tinpot cabaret that time forgot in Paris. And this girl.

No, she didn't come with ownership papers—more was the pity. Khaled smiled privately to himself.

'Is that really how you ended up with us?'

He glanced her way, almost literally tripping over that shy look she was so good at giving him.

It just muddied the waters—had him wanting to lecture her on coming up to a stranger's hotel room and at the same time wanting to drive her down backwards onto this sofa, scatter the cushions and reacquaint himself with the sweet, sensual response she'd given him in the bedroom.

He cleared his throat. 'I have a regular poker game with a group of guys I've known since my army days.'

'Where you got those terrible scars?'

'*Da*—some.'

It hadn't been a smart move showing her those scars. It had led to her hands on his body and his on hers.

Khaled slumped back on the sofa beside her and massaged the back of his neck, wondering what the hell he thought he was doing and knowing he had to wind this up.

'How long did you serve?' she wanted to know.

'Two years.'

'I guess you saw active service?'

'Chechnya, Afghanistan,' he said briefly, and a visual of heat and dust and sweat streaming between the bridge of his nose and a rifle sight bloomed in his mind. God, how he'd hated it.

'Was it your choice?'

Khaled gave a shrug, a little surprised by the question. Few people asked. 'It's difficult to escape conscription—but, yes, in many ways it was my choice. My father was a professional soldier.'

She sat forward and tucked one leg under her. Clearly interested.

'Did you want to follow him into the army?'

'Talkative little thing, aren't you?'

'I'm just curious.'

He could give her the truth, that military service had opened up his life in unexpected ways and had transformed his life. He'd learned that his father was a hero, that he came from a long line of professional soldiers, and that his own beliefs about who he was and where he came from had been false and fed to him as a youth by the only father he had ever known. Leaving him with the huge trust issues he carried to this day.

But he opted for the generic. 'It's something we must all do.'

Her world of feathers and stage make-up was so far from what he'd seen as to be another planet. And yet he couldn't help remembering those marks he'd seen on her feet, and the way she'd curled up like a snail on the vanity to hide them.

He frowned. Mostly it was his own fiercely protective re-action that continued to unsettle him, especially when he'd learned that some of that violence had been meted out by what sounded like a disgrace of a father.

'Military service is boredom punctuated by adrenalin,'

he found himself confessing. 'And a lot of poker. I got very good at it.' He angled a smile her way. 'When I was a kid I used to play cards for spent bullet cartridges.'

Hell, why had he told her *that*?

'Bullets, huh? I guess where you come from is a long way from the dressing rooms and trailers I was raised in.' She looked up at him through her lashes. 'You'd probably prefer them to a cabaret you don't want.'

'I don't know,' he mused, unable to resist the siren call of her eyes shyly meeting his. 'I wouldn't have met you.'

Her mouth trembled into a half-smile and then she pulled it tight again, looking away. He knew the feeling.

He rubbed his jaw, knowing he should be winding this up—only to encounter the beard he'd ignored for weeks now. Usually after a couple of months away on a trek he'd be freshly shaven and snapped back into his Italian suits, hunkering down in his offices in Moscow and hitting the ground running.

Diverting to Paris straight from the Arctic shelf meant he'd come without that symbolic shift between two worlds.

Maybe that was why he was tempting fate here. The wilderness of his previous environment was still running through his blood...

He cleared his throat. 'Gigi, in the bedroom—'

'I don't want to talk about it.' She cut him off hurriedly, looking cornered. She stumbled to her feet. 'I mean, it was just a stupid thing, right? Better we forget about it.'

A stupid thing? He didn't think so. His hunter's instinct kicked in.

Gigi set about clumsily gathering her things. 'I should get out of your hair.'

'I'm taking you home.'

The words formed and his certainty solidified around them.

'No, that's all right.' She was busily packing up her laptop.

'I'm taking you home.'

Gigi tried to ignore the little kick she got out of his assertiveness. Because, really, she shouldn't like being told what to do.

But she could literally hear her heart hammering in her ears, and more liquid heat was pooling between her thighs. It was embarrassing. It was also unprecedented in *The Romantic History of Gigi Valente*. So far officially two pages, along with today's Special Addition, and not much going on for the foreseeable future.

She couldn't understand the effect this man—of all men—had on her.

Obviously he had it all going on. He was gorgeous, he was powerful, and his fathoms-deep masculine voice with that accent was designed to be meltingly effective on a woman's hormones...

But if she had to pinpoint it she'd say it was in his eyes and the way he looked at her. As if he wanted to do all kinds of things with her that another woman would slap him for, and that instead made *her* feel beautiful and female and, yes, fluttery.

She just wasn't a fluttery kind of girl.

She zipped her finger into the backpack.

Ouch!

Shoving her middle finger in her mouth, she tried not to look at him. He was being so reasonable, which wasn't helping, and now he wanted to drive her home.

Didn't he understand that if she spent any more time with him she might very well push him down, climb on top of him and make him kiss her all over again?

Or, worse, make him stroke her breasts—because her nipples were like tight little marbles and they felt tingly, and she only had to close her eyes to remember how it had felt to be pressed up into his big hands...

She swallowed hard and kept her head down.

'You don't need to drive me home.' She slung the backpack over her shoulder. 'I can grab a taxi.'

Actually, she would find a *vélib* station and bike it home. Taxis were for rich people, or girls who danced at the Lido.

She adjusted the strap on her backpack to give herself something to do when he didn't reply. Raised her eyes. He was looking down at her as if she'd said something bizarre, and then he flashed her a scarily intimate look that told her he knew exactly how damp her knickers were.

'You're only saying that because you haven't seen my car.'

CHAPTER NINE

'TAKE A LEFT up here and we're at the top of the street.'

Khaled didn't know what he'd expected. Something tight on space and utilitarian, given the area. Montmartre had come a long way from the fields and cheap lodgings of its artistic heyday. Apartment dwelling wasn't cheap in these parts. And he'd seen what the showgirls were paid—it wasn't a lucrative profession.

He hadn't expected the little dead-end cobbled street, the high grey stone walls or the four-storeyed *petit mansion* peering overhead.

He parked his yellow Spyder Lamborghini on the roadside between a couple of not inconsiderably priced cars and eased back to take a look at Gigi.

'This is it?'

She was taking off her belt. 'Sure.'

He watched her for a moment, running her hand over the door, trying to get out. She appeared to be in a hurry. He could have leaned across and done it for her. Instead he opened his own door and strolled around to her side of the car. He lifted the door and watched her get out, taking in those incredible legs and the pert roundness of her behind.

'Thanks.' She lugged her backpack over her shoulder. 'Are you coming up?'

'Do you usually let men you hardly know into your flat?'

She gave him a surprised look, as if it hadn't occurred to her before, and then reached into her jacket and brought out a small tube, brandishing it like a gunslinger.

'I'm packing heat.'

'What's that?' He took it from her, examining the simple pump-style device.

'A high-frequency alarm. All the girls at the cabaret have them.'

'I take it this was the Dantons' idea.'

She shook her head. 'Jacques considers what we do off the clock our own business—he's not big on the health and safety thing. But some of the girls have had problems with patrons following them when they leave the theatre, so I got Martin to introduce a courtesy bus system, which is great. Lulu and I use that all the time.'

'Who supplied the alarms?'

'Me. I got one for Lulu, after she was almost attacked one night, and grabbed one for myself too. The guy who sold them to me gave me a discount for a box of two dozen. So I got enough for the other girls.'

'Basically, you're doing the Dantons' job for them?'

Her expressive face gave her away. She obviously didn't want to down-talk the cabaret's management in front of him, but at the same time it was fairly clear what was going on.

'I guess if something needs to be done you do it, right? Besides, Lulu could have been in real trouble that night.'

'One of the dancers was attacked?' Khaled was frowning.

'Not "one of the dancers",' she said, with a little frown to match his. '*Lulu*. She went out with this guy a couple of times, and then she said thanks but no thanks, and he followed her home and wouldn't take no for an answer. If I hadn't been here I don't know what would have happened.'

Her natural animation had drained away and she folded her arms across her chest self-protectively. 'Plus we work at night, so personal security is pretty important. You can't be in this business without learning how to look out for yourself.'

'You carry a small alarm,' he said, struggling with primitive feelings that had no place here, with a girl who was certainly of a time and a place where she could look after herself, 'and you think this is security enough?'

'It's all I've got,' she replied simply.

He made a note to himself to beef up security at L'Oiseau Bleu. The cabaret he wouldn't be holding on to.

At the gate she keyed in the alarm code and pushed.

The courtyard was small and immaculate.

A black mop came hurtling across the stones to fling itself at Gigi's knees. She swept the ball up in her arms amidst much unhygienic kissing and cooing.

'This is Coco—he's Lulu's baby. Say hello, Coco.'

Khaled watched this interaction with a degree of mild male apprehension.

Normally women who treated defenceless animals as substitute children really didn't do it for him, and surely it was a warning sign that at some point this roving maternal instinct was going to be turned in a more natural direction.

But that was some other guy's problem. He could relax about the dog. It wasn't even her dog.

Forget about the dog.

'Here. You hold Coco while I let us in.' She shoved the fluff ball at his chest.

Khaled tensed. *It's a dog, not a baby,* he reiterated, and held the creature up, observing its shiny eyes, wet nose and glossy coat. Coco was clearly in good health and well looked after. He lifted the squirming ball a little higher and confirmed that Coco was indeed a he.

Gigi opened the front door and he put the dog down. It rushed forward and up the stairs.

'We're on the top floor,' she said, crossing the well-lit atrium and preceding him up the steps.

We? How the hell did she afford this on her wages? She barely made enough at that cabaret to live in a cardboard box in central Paris. He knew—he'd seen the books.

But his eyes were caught by Gigi's small round derrière, several steps in front of him and right on his eye level, and all the questions got pushed aside in favour of just appreciating the view. Her bottom should be illegal. In those jeans it was packaged for maximum impact. The soft denim wrapped around her as if it loved her body. He couldn't blame it.

He followed her into a brightly lit open-plan room with

windows looking out over the rooftops. It was a nice view. The floorboards shone. There was a loft bedroom above and circular metal stairs.

Gigi shrugged off her jacket and tossed it onto a chair.

His mouth dried up.

He hadn't got much of a look when she'd been under him on the bed, but now he could see the full effect of a tight pink T-shirt advertising the slogan 'Dancing Queen' in glittery dark pink letters across the high round curves of her breasts.

He'd had those breasts resting against his hands, felt the curve of her nipples rise to points under his thumbs.

She looked lovely and playful—and so sexy it hurt.

The blood zoomed so fast from his brain to his groin he could only be thankful he'd put his jacket on.

'Dancing Queen?' he said, a little stupidly.

Gigi glanced down at her chest, looked up, and beamed like a torch.

'I love Abba. Want a cup of tea?'

'*Chay*…tea?' he echoed. He never drank tea. '*Spasiba.*'

He knew he should be pounding down those stairs and driving away. Didn't he have meetings this afternoon? Instead he found himself moving around the room while she busied herself in the kitchenette, taking in the simple furnishings and girly throw cushions, the pile of books beside a small bookcase that had overflowed, a couple of framed prints that under closer inspection proved to be old numbers of *Le Petit Journal*, with illustrations of dancing girls—one from the Moulin Rouge, the other from a circus. No sign of male cohabitation.

She was saying something about the cabaret…about wanting to show him some memorabilia.

He drew closer to a twelve-by-twelve photographic portrait framed on the wall. For a moment he thought it was Gigi. The same sharp angular cheekbones were catching the light, the point of her chin, but the eyes were dark and sloe-shaped, the nose small. The face was more conventionally attractive, but lacking the energy which animated Gigi's striking features. Struck by the similarity to the woman with him, the last thing he noticed was that she appeared to be naked. Except for an ostrich feather fan.

'This is your mother?' he said.

Gigi put down the cups she was setting out and came over, settling her gaze on the picture with an oddly protective look on her face.

'That's right. Her name was Emily Fitzgerald. She danced at L'Oiseau Bleu for five years—same as me.'

'Your mother was a showgirl?' Khaled gave a soft laugh. 'Well, well…'

'She was amazing. A much better dancer than me. She had real presence. Those fans she's holding she had made for her. They were her signature. They weigh a ton. I know, because they were the only thing she took back to Dublin, the fans—oh, and her shoes. I used to waddle around in her shoes, trying to carry one of the fans. I couldn't have been more than five or six. She said if I practised I could grow up to be another Sally Rand.'

'Who was Sally Rand?'

'An American burlesque star—famous for dancing naked behind an ostrich feather fan. She started out in the circus too.'

She spoke so matter-of-factly that Khaled decided not to raise the subject of all this pointing towards a rather unusual upbringing.

'I gather your mother gave up the stage to have a family?'

Gigi's mouth tightened. 'You could say that. She fell pregnant to my father. Not the most reliable man in the world,' she added.

Khaled thought of the marks on her feet and decided this was Gigi's version of understatement.

'She decided to go home to her parents and I was born in Dublin. I didn't know my dad until I was eight or nine.' She reached out and straightened the picture, although it was already dead on. 'This photo was taken when she was pregnant with me. She had it done knowing her time was running out. She kept dancing right up until she started to show.'

'Do showgirls come back to work after pregnancy?' He had no real interest, but he wanted to hear her story—because it was clear that here on this wall was the reason Gigi was so anxious to protect the cabaret.

'If your body snaps back. A couple of the dancers have kids. The Dantons aren't great about childcare.' She folded her arms. 'That's something else you might want to look into.'

In truth Khaled had forgotten this was the bone of contention between them. He'd been enjoying watching all the emotions crossing Gigi's face, like sunlight and cloud and little storms. She was so passionate.

He looked again at the photograph. Emily Fitzgerald looked serene as a sunset.

'She must be proud of you.'

'She doesn't know. She died.' A muscle jumped in Gigi's throat. 'She went into hospital for a day procedure, to fix some nodules that had formed on her larynx, and she never came out from under the anaesthetic. It was her heart—it was weak and no one knew, and it just gave up. It was sixteen years ago, but it's still hard to grapple with.'

She'd been just a child.

Khaled straightened. His voice was gravel. 'I'm sorry, Gigi.'

He had the unfamiliar sensation of not quite knowing his footing here. But this girl did that to him.

His own parents had been gone by the time he was thirteen, and it had given him a terrible freedom.

He frowned. 'What happened to you?'

'My dad turned up to collect me.' She put her hands on her hips, as if to counteract the wealth unsaid in that statement. 'That's when I went on the road with Valente's International Circus.'

'An itinerant life for a kid… Did you enjoy it?'

She shrugged. 'It was different. I threw myself into learning the life. I so wanted to please my dad, and it taught me lessons in discipline and the importance of practice.'

Khaled had a visual of the marks on her feet, and those words assumed a darker significance.

It wasn't hard to picture Gigi all those years ago, skinny instead of shapely, all freckles and bereft. They weren't so different. He knew all about trying to please the only person you had left. In Gigi's case it had involved climbing those ropes, her feet bearing the scars to this day.

Tough little thing.

Needing her mother and getting what…? The bastard who'd permitted that *thing* to happen to her growing feet.

Khaled was conscious of a tension in him he could have cut with a knife.

'Then Dad went bankrupt and we hit the vaudeville circuit,' she continued. 'I sang and danced and dad was MC. But it wasn't like this.'

She gestured towards the window and he surmised that she meant Parisian cabaret.

'As soon as I could I crossed the Channel.'

'You came to Paris to follow in her footsteps?'

'Something like that.'

She smiled at him, and it was that lack of self-pity coupled with her natural buoyancy that hit him the hardest. He was sure he could do something for her before he left Paris.

'Would you like that tea?' she asked.

'No, I don't want tea.' He stepped in front of her. 'I want to kiss you.'

She looked sweetly surprised, and then pleased, and it only made him want to power her back into that sofa over there and lose himself in her soft, sweet warmth. He took her in his arms and promised himself he'd only have a taste. But once her lips parted beneath his everything changed again, and his kiss became a fiercely possessive gesture that only

ntensified as her tongue tentatively slid against his. His
Dlood roared and his restraint began to unravel fast.

The door behind him closed with a slam.

Gigi jerked in his arms, her head coming up. She made
a sound of dismay that might have been funny if she hadn't
then shoved him away from her and immediately begun
smoothing down her hair and adjusting her T-shirt, looking
guilty as hell and incredibly sexy because of it.

Which wasn't helping with the stone-cold kick he needed
to give his erection.

Because the little brunette from yesterday was standing
just inside the door, with a bunch of sunflowers and a bag
of groceries. She dropped them on the floor.

It wasn't subtle. It wasn't meant to be.

'I'm interrupting,' she said stonily.

'No…' choked Gigi.

His personal phone vibrated inside his jacket for the hun-
dredth time since he'd driven the Spyder out into the Paris
afternoon. He thought he'd take this call. It had been a lot
of years since he'd involved himself with a woman who had
a *flatmate*.

Khaled palmed his phone and turned his back on the girls
to give them a minute. *'Govorit,'* he breathed. *Talk.*

'What is *he* doing here?' hissed Lulu, stepping over the groceries.

Gigi opted for a casual shrug. She had no idea how she
was going to explain two hundred plus pounds of Russian
muscle in their flat, let alone her being welded to him. She
had her own questions as to why she'd practically blurted
out her entire family history to him.

Lulu looked very angry. She marched into her bedroom.
Reluctantly Gigi trailed her.

'So you're replacing Solange?' she demanded as Gigi half
shut the door behind her.

'No!' Gigi frowned. 'It's not like that. He was never interested in Solange.'

Lulu gave a very un-Lulu-like snort. '*Every* man's interested in Solange.'

Gigi's stomach curled uneasily. It was true. 'He told me it was a publicity thing—to have his photograph taken with a showgirl.'

Her best friend's face told her what she thought of that.

'So what are you doing here with him, Gigi? How did this come about?'

She told Lulu about being tackled by his security team, about running through the streets, being held up by aggressive strangers and swarmed by paparazzi. When she'd finished Lulu's mouth was slightly ajar. She shut it with a snap when Gigi came to the part about going up to his hotel room.

'He took me up to fix my feet.'

'You let him see your *feet*?' Lulu's voice rose.

'Shh. He'll hear you. Don't make it such a big deal.' Although it *was* a big deal. Lulu knew that better than most. 'We happened to be in the bathroom.'

'How were you in the bathroom together?'

'He carried me there.'

Lulu's eyes narrowed suspiciously. 'What happened to your ability to walk?'

'It was compromised by my blisters.'

Her best friend gave her a withering look.

Gigi decided there and then to omit the part about her turning into a nympho on the vanity. Some things were private—and, besides, Lulu wouldn't understand. The only time *she* got carried away by her hormones was when they watched old Gregory Peck movies together, and Lulu would hug a cushion and sigh and ask where all the real men had gone.

Gigi suspected she had one, in the other room, but letting Lulu know that wasn't going to help.

After all she'd said about him over the last couple of days, she couldn't blame Lulu for being suspicious.

'I gave him the presentation and he seemed interested. Then he ran me home because of the journalists.' Even as she said it, it sounded weak.

He'd brought her home and effectively diverted her from her task, which had been to show him the old memorabilia, by asking her about her mother.

Then he'd kissed her. Tenderly at first. She touched her lips.

Lulu's eyes zeroed in on the gesture and her expression turned mutinous. 'Has he even said anything about the caba-ret? Or is this all just about getting in a showgirl's knickers?'

Lulu blushed as she said it, but she said it nonetheless.

'It's not like that!'

Lulu folded her arms. '"Nobody should date Kitaev"— quote, unquote.'

'I know…I know.'

Lulu's expression softened to its more natural lines. 'Gigi, just think for a minute. How are you going to explain any of this to the other girls?'

'The other girls won't know.'

The words just slipped out, and Gigi knew then that she was sunk.

'You want to do this behind everyone's backs? Really, Gigi?'

'No, of course not.'

Lulu knew about her past. Knew how fiercely she felt about deceit.

Her father had put her on the vaudeville circuit at the age of fourteen—a front for his petty crime spree as they trav-elled from town to town. And four years later, when she'd confronted him outside the court on that rainy day when he'd been convicted and she'd got a slap over the wrist, he'd told her that he hadn't thought it would matter as long as she didn't know…

Ignorance wasn't an excuse for culpability under the law—she knew that now, better than most.

She'd made a vow when she'd walked away from court that morning seven years ago that she was going to look life straight in the eye.

She looked Lulu in the eye now. 'It won't happen again.'

She couldn't promote the theatre and compromise her position.

The world could be a cold, hard place, but you didn't need to cheat and steal to survive in it. She had fought to make her own colourful, *honest* corner and she wasn't going to mess it up now.

Khaled was still talking on his phone when she re-emerged. Lulu followed her, arms folded. He indicated the door with a nod and headed out, clearly expecting her to follow him.

'Do *not* make any plans with him,' whispered Lulu.

No, no plans.

Outside on the stairs he pocketed his phone and said briefly, 'We've got a problem.'

'Yes, we do.'

She had a huge problem, given she still couldn't pull her eyes off him. But she was guessing it wasn't such a big problem for him, because she was looking at his back and he was taking the steps by threes, those big shoulders squared as he headed back out into the big, bad world.

'There are photographs of us in the lobby of the Plaza.'

That wasn't the problem she'd been thinking of, but... 'Okay...'

Because, really, what did he want her to say? She was sorry, but she had told him she was happy to go on her way. *He* was the one who'd gone all he-man over fixing up her feet. Her heart performed a little tumble and roll at the thought.

'No, it's *not* okay, Gigi.' He stopped at the bottom of the stairs and turned around. His expression was taut. 'They imply a sexual relationship.'

Gigi rocked back on her heels. Okay. She could deal with that. Just. The other girls were going to kill her, but it wasn't the end of the world. Was it?

She examined his fierce expression. Told herself she wasn't bothered that he seemed to think this was a disaster. I mean, some guys actually thought she was pretty hot stuff. She might not be beating them off with a stick, like most of the other girls, but she got asked out, a lot...and if she wasn't working most evenings she'd probably go...

'I suggest you don't step onstage for the next few nights.'

What had he just said?

'But that's impossible!'

'*Nyet*, it's very possible. You need to keep a low profile—although after today it's probably asking the impossible.'

'What's that supposed to mean?'

He leaned against the banister, effectively keeping her on the second to last step, which gave her a slight height advantage although he still made her feel tiny.

'*Dushka*, you're a walking headline right now.'

'Excuse me? There were *two* of us on the Champs-Élysées, and you were the one attracting all the attention. All I did was speak up for you.'

He looked at her with those unfathomable dark eyes. 'Yes, you did, and if you'd kept your mouth shut you'd just be the pretty, unidentified girl in some photographs of me out jogging. But you're a Bluebird, and you announced it to the whole world.'

He looked over her shoulder, up the flight of stairs, and Gigi turned around to see Lulu standing on the landing, arms folded.

Oh, honestly! Gigi jumped down the final two steps and headed confidently for the door. Lulu couldn't spy on them if they were outside.

Khaled's arm came down in front of her, effectively barring the door.

'Being seen in public together probably isn't our wisest step at this point,' he said, with calm certainty.

She looked up. 'But this isn't *public*. This is my street.'

'Nevertheless, there could be paps—stay put.'

She folded her arms, looking away. 'Fine.'

His mouth moved as if he were suppressing a smile and he picked up the ends of her hair and gave the silky weight a gentle tug, which felt oddly more intimate than that kiss upstairs.

'No more ambushing men in hotel lobbies, *dushka*.'

She bit her lip and gazed up at him, fighting the urge to move a little closer.

He dropped her hair as if he'd just realised what he was doing and cleared his throat. 'Next time you have a proposal to put forward pick up the phone and make an appointment.'

Gigi nodded, although she knew very well that if she *had* picked up the phone she never would have got anywhere near him.

Not the man who was solidifying to granite rock in front of her eyes.

This was the man she'd first seen yesterday—a monolith of inaccessibility. The open-necked shirt and jeans might as well have been a suit.

She guessed that if he'd been wearing a watch he'd be glancing at it.

A busy man, with places to be and people to do his bidding.

It was disconcerting to think she'd been kissing him upstairs not so long ago, but it helped her suddenly fragile ego to remind herself that there hadn't been anything inaccessible about the way he'd been acting then. It wasn't just her imagination. He'd been moulding his hands around her bottom and bringing her in tight against his erection. You couldn't fake that.

She hugged to herself the very female knowledge that he'd been putty in her hands for a few minutes there.

'So, will you keep in mind everything I've shown you?'

Her words prompted Khaled's attention to drop to her breasts. When he realised what he was doing he dragged his gaze away from her nipples, prominent against the T-shirt fabric between those glittery letters, and gritted his teeth.

He had to stop making this sexual—he *would* defeat it. Gigi was looking up at him as if she expected something from him. Only it wasn't sexual. She was still holding out hope for that damn cabaret.

He looked down into her anxious expression and almost told her the truth. He was selling up. She'd come to the wrong man. But the minute he did that all of Paris would know and the queue of prospective buyers would evaporate.

He did, however, want to do something for her before he walked out of her life. 'Have you thought about upscaling?'

'Upscaling?' She gave a nervous laugh. 'It sounds like a disease.'

'Paris is full of venues. Isn't the Lido still going strong?'

'Why are you talking about the Lido? I'd never get into the Lido.'

'I could pull a few strings…'

She pulled her generous mouth tight. He was beginning to recognise the gesture.

'That's not why I came to see you today. I don't need a handout. I came for the cabaret.'

'It's not a handout, Gigi, it's a word in someone's ear. It happens all the time.'

'Well, I don't want underhand things going on.'

Underhand? Khaled tried not to laugh, but she looked so indignant. 'Gigi, how did you get the job at L'Oiseau Bleu?'

'I tried out.'

'Did you mention your mother?'

'Yes.'

'Nepotism.'

She put her hands on her hips. 'I'll have you know I'm the best showgirl they've got. I earned my place on talent alone.'

He tried not to smile, given she'd unintentionally stuck her chest out. He was tempted to point out that a significant part of her job relied on the talent that filled out her bra, but their interaction could only go downhill from that point.

She clearly prided herself on her job.

'Then you should have no problem with the Lido.'

Gigi made an exasperated sound.

They were going round in circles and, he recognised, they were talking about different things. Her heart was in L'Oiseau Bleu.

But Gigi's loyalty was misplaced and she couldn't see it. He suspected she was blinded by that photograph on the wall upstairs.

She was trying to reclaim something that had never existed instead of looking at the facts.

He had always looked long and hard at the reality of things.

The fatherless boy who wasn't wanted had hardened into a man who understood that human relationships would always fail you. What you could rely upon was money in the bank and the things you built with your own hands.

But it was proving difficult to dwell on the harsh reality of things with Gigi standing in front of him, vibrating with passion and determination to have her way.

Khaled recognised that he was possibly behaving like every other man who'd crossed her path—being foolishly helpful towards her because he was slightly bowled over by her personality.

She *did* offer a powerful punch of sex appeal.

It was nicely packaged too, in tight jeans, and advertised with that glittery slogan stretched across her perky breasts.

He was tempted to give way to instinct and just take her. Throw her over his shoulder and get the hell out of Paris.

It was what his ancestors would have done.

It wouldn't be what she wanted. She was clearly happy where she was, but what she wanted was the impossible.

Even if he recharged the cabaret's batteries with money there were so many other variables to consider.

When he was younger he'd thought money and success would shift things, make life somehow easier. Naturally the little things, like domestic service—knowing that his clothes would always be pressed, a car waiting for him—made the wheels turn smoother, but the bigger tests in life remained. They just assumed larger and in some cases—as in this weekend in Paris—absurd proportions.

He was being attacked for being moneyed and successful and foreign.

But you couldn't change what people had decided to think about you.

He knew that better than most.

It was a fact he was fighting right now, in his efforts to get that road in down south.

He exhaled, the weight of the world shifting once more onto his shoulders and the weariness he'd been keeping at bay with work making itself known. Truth be told, he wouldn't mind just climbing into bed with Gigi for a week in this little flat in Montmartre. Ditch the friend and any reminders of the cabaret and work out this scorching lust until both of them were exhausted and he was bored and it was time to move on.

His gaze ran over her creamy freckle-dappled skin, the curve of her lower lip, noticed the faint blush of colour in her cheeks. He cleared his throat and said, 'Keep offstage tonight—do that for me.'

Gigi muttered something about pay being docked and Paris being an expensive city.

He wanted to shake her.

He wanted even more to slide his hand around her sinuous waist under the T-shirt and feel her body temperature rise, to have the points of her breasts brush against him and take

her mouth and plunder it until she was making those sound.
he suspected would rise tenfold when he was inside her.

Instead, what he said was, 'I'll put in a word. When you
get an audition, take it.'

CHAPTER TEN

KHALED MIGHT HAVE had a point about staying offstage, but for an entirely different reason, Gigi realised that evening as she faced twenty-two hostile dancers in the narrow confines of the dressing room.

'You sold us out, you cow,' said Leah.

They had just come offstage, and Gigi found herself surrounded by a lot of hot, riled-up girls who'd had to run the same gauntlet of media she had when they'd come in tonight. The atmosphere was slightly hysterical, to say the least.

'What happened to all that talk about him being the enemy?' demanded Trixie.

'You just wanted him for yourself,' said Adele.

'It's always the quiet ones,' said Solange, narrowing her green eyes, and there was a lot of murmuring in agreement.

Gigi folded her arms. 'Well, *that's* not true—I never shut up!'

Her attempt to lighten the mood went nowhere.

'Quiet, Valente. You're in trouble,' said Susie, levelling her with a look. 'We all know what's going on out front, and you can bet the headlines tomorrow aren't going to be about the show. It'll be wall-to-wall reports on how the Bluebirds are giving it up to the billionaire.'

'What did he promise you?' Inez wanted to know.

Gigi's mind flashed to the Lido and she reddened.

'After everything you said, Gigi!' cried Trixie reproachfully. 'I can't believe you'd sell us out.'

'I didn't! I tried to get him on side.'

'It's one rule for her, girls, and one for us,' said Leah contemptuously.

'I've got a bloody audition at the Moulin Rouge next week,' said Susie suddenly. 'If this stuffs it up for me I'm coming after you, Valente.'

'The *Moulin Rouge*?' chorused several of the girls, head turning.

'Why?' piped up Adele.

'Why do you think?' Susie folded her arms. 'Gigi's right about one thing: this ship's going down fast. Probably a lot faster now, with half of the French media out front, zeroing in on what a hokey show we put on. Add in the hated Russian owner living it up in a hotel with one of the Bluebirds and we're the joke of Paris!'

'What's she talking about?' asked Trixie. 'We've got a full house tonight.'

'That's only tonight,' Susie scoffed. 'Kitaev isn't going to hang on to us. He'll hand this place over to the Conseil de Paris, it'll be heritage-listed and you know what that means—we'll all be out on our *derrières*.'

Gigi frowned. 'Who told you that?'

'What else is he going to do? He won't be able to sell the place now. We're a joke.'

The other girls were humming with consternation. A couple were glaring at Susie, but Gigi knew she wasn't off the hook.

Sensing the shift in hostility, Susie turned her way again and looked her up and down contemptuously. '*You*, Valente, have turned us into a joke. Why don't you ask your new boyfriend what he's got planned, Gigi? Or are you too busy dropping your knickers for him at the Plaza Athénée?'

Heads swivelled Gigi's way again, effectively pushing Susie's defection to the side—which had clearly been her intention.

Gigi almost told them that her knickers had stayed very firmly in place, only that wasn't entirely true. They'd slipped... But she didn't want to think about that right now.

Fed up, she picked up her things and shouldered her way out of the room. At least she'd tried!

Barricading herself in the second dressing room, she

checked her phone. She'd been too chicken until now. For good reason, it turned out. The girls were right. It was all over the internet. Photos of her and Khaled in the street, an 'eyewitness account' of them in the lobby of his hotel. Even a shot of him climbing into his car on her street.

Kitaev and feathered friend!

No wonder those journalists had been yelling her name out front.

Gigi said a bad word and shoved her phone into her change bag.

Wonderful. She was officially the Bluebird who'd sold out—not just in the eyes of her troupe mates but in the opinion of the rest of Paris!

It was all she could think about as she waited in the wings for her next cue.

Because right now she had to go out there and perform in front of people who believed she was some sort of Mata Hari. What on earth did people think? That she'd traded sexual favours for...what? Job security?

A sort of shock was stealing over her. She'd had such good intentions, and yet in the span of a single day she'd lost everyone's respect, probably her job, and risked any future jobs. And what happened to the cabaret was anyone's guess.

It wasn't Khaled's fault. Gigi knew she'd walked into this on her own two feet. But as she did her best not to fall apart so close to stage time she couldn't help feeling his exit this afternoon meant she'd been hung out to dry.

'I'm looking for Gigi Valente,' Khaled told the first stage-hand he found.

The kid just stared at him, bug-eyed. 'She's j-just gone onstage, Mr Kitaev,' he stammered.

His driver hadn't been able to get the SUV within a block

of the entrance to the theatre tonight. There were protesters picketing on the pavement, and the media presence spilling onto the road was causing traffic mayhem. He'd also seen that the billboard advertising the show out front had been defaced with graffiti.

The police had been throwing up a blockade as he'd arrived.

And Gigi had chosen to go onstage.

'What the hell are those idiot brothers thinking?' he snarled, and the kid jumped, but Khaled was already making his way out into the audience.

He'd fed Gigi's name into an internet search engine this afternoon. It turned out that Gisele Valente had a charlatan for a father—which wasn't surprising, given what she'd already told him. But what she had neglected to mention was her own role in his all-singing and all-dancing revue as the Valentes had travelled the English provinces, ripping off the punters.

A grainy photograph of Gigi aged eighteen outside court, with a physically imposing, defiant-looking middle-aged man sent mixed feelings through him. He'd seen her scars, and he knew enough of her story to know she hadn't had it easy, but she'd purposely left out the part about her being her father's accomplice.

It was a neat little con, and he had to wonder what she was up to now.

Although as he took in once more the faded glamour of the theatre he had to acknowledge that she'd achieved something this afternoon. The cabaret did look different to him after her presentation. She might not have sold him on the place, but her proposal had gone a lot further than all the media-manufactured ire of Paris and the bumbling excuses of the Danton brothers to bring him on side.

Speaking of which, the Danton brothers, alerted to his presence, were on his heels.

L'Oiseau Bleu had its first full house in months, according to an excitable Jacques Danton. They'd never seen anything like it.

'Mr Kitaev, we know members of the press are in the audience, but we can't do anything about it if they have tickets.'

Martin Danton was wringing his hands as Khaled shouldered his way along the perimeter of the auditorium.

'Who sold them tickets?'

There was an uncomfortable to-ing and fro-ing between the brothers.

Buffoons.

Onstage an act was in full swing, involving the tank he'd seen yesterday being put to a different use. Tonight it was full of bubbling water, like a cauldron, and inside two monstrous Burmese pythons glided to and fro.

There was also a girl in there, but he hadn't been paying it much attention, more interested in finding Gigi as unobtrusively as possible. Where the hell was she?

Impatiently he glanced at his watch. He didn't have time for this.

His attention was diverted when he noticed one of the monsters appeared to have wrapped itself around the swimming girl and was dragging her down to the base of the tank.

'Is that monitored?' he snarled.

'A handler is ready to intervene if there's a problem, Mr Kitaev,' Jacques Danton scrambled to assure him.

'It looks like they *are* having a problem. Those snakes—what size are they?'

'Almost three m-metres,' stuttered Martin Danton.

'Then they're capable of crushing the life out of a human being.'

'Only a *small* human being,' Jacques Danton countered, 'and Gigi is a robust girl—she's stronger than she looks.'

Gigi?

Khaled shoved the smaller man out of his path and made

his way to the stage. He was about to breach the safety rail when the swimmer broke free and shot through the water, breaking the surface to emerge gracefully from the tank, seemingly no worse for wear, dripping water.

It was Gigi, all right. Painted gold from neck to toes, with the lights strobing over her body and the music as seductive as any snake-charmer's medley.

She was also naked.

There was an appreciative intake of breath from the audience as she struck a pose and the lights slid over her gold painted body in what was frankly an erotic tribute.

Only Gigi posed as if she was the star attraction that she was.

From the darkness of the audience came a shout, 'Kitaev's whore!'

He went cold, and then something hot and virulent licked up inside him.

Gigi, instead of vacating the stage, had climbed down from her perch and begun to search the darkness for the origin of the slur.

In a moment she had gone from glorious, sensual goddess bewitching her audience, to the sturdily game girl who had chased him down the Champs-Élysées and stood up to his detractors like Liberté defending her people.

Khaled had already discovered he really liked that girl.

It galvanised him.

He vaulted up onto the stage, stepped over the footlights and strode towards her. Gigi's expression was one of total bewilderment as she saw him coming.

That's right, his id growled, *worrying about me is the first smart thing you've done all night.*

Such was her shock, she didn't so much as utter a squeak as he hoisted her up over his shoulder. She only began to struggle and scissor her legs as they came offstage, shouting something about him being a madman and telling him to put her down and that he'd ruined the act.

On the contrary—this felt like the sanest he'd been in years.

Gigi was quickly made aware that they were headed for the exit, with her riding his shoulder like a surfboard, through a sea of gaping showgirls, past gawping stagehands and their own security men, Jules and Jean, who made no attempt to stop him.

'Put me down!' she shouted. 'Are you crazy?'

'Da.'

'Where are you taking me?'

'Out of harm's way.' He said this as if it were obvious.

'Put me back onstage, Mr Kitaev. I have a show to do!'

'Mr Kitaev?' he growled.

'I think we should be professional at work.'

'Your work—not mine.'

'I refuse to go with you!'

'Bad luck. You're not climbing back in that tank.'

'It's my act!'

'Tonight Paris wants to drown you, and those idiot brothers thought it was a good idea to put you in a tank of water in front of them?'

'Nobody wants to drown me except the other girls, and now you've just made it worse!'

He kept going.

'You can't just carry me out of here. What are people going to say?'

'The same thing they're already saying,' he snarled, as if this was the last thing he wanted. 'That I can't keep my hands off you.'

There was shouting behind them, but Khaled was kicking open the exit door.

'You can't take me out of here—I'm naked!' she shrieked.

'Yes,' Khaled said, and he didn't sound happy about it, 'you *are*.'

The cold air and the night rushed at her, and then she was being lifted into a waiting SUV.

Khaled leapt in after her and the door slammed. They took off at speed.

Gigi scrunched herself up against the opposite door, arms plastered across her chest, legs crossed, horribly aware that she was practically naked, covered in gold paint and dripping wet. Humiliated.

'Are you *insane*?' she exploded.

He reached for her and she began kicking out at him with her feet.

'Don't you touch me, you pervert! You're a madman!'

One of her six-inch stilettos caught against the denim of his jeans and tipped the shoe off her foot. He grasped her other foot and yanked off the second glittery shoe, whisked down the window and threw both of them out into the passing night.

Gigi watched on in utter disbelief.

'Those shoes are the property of L'Oiseau Bleu! They're hand-made!'

'There are paparazzi crawling all over that theatre,' he snarled, as if this were *her* fault, and she retreated like a turtle who had stuck its neck out and almost had it cut off—before she realised he was holding a phone in one hand while warding off her pummelling feet with the other. 'I want to know how and why they got into the building.'

He pocketed his phone and sat forward, to shrug his big shoulders out of his wool coat.

'The paps will have photographs of us, but they can't do any more damage.'

'It was you they wanted!'

'Don't be so naïve,' he growled, 'and stop hammering me with your feet.'

'Then let me out of this car.' She gave him another inef-

fectual shove with the soles of her feet, but with no real conviction, only to have him throw his coat over her.

'What are you doing?' she demanded as he began to feed
one of her flailing arms into a sleeve.

'Keeping you warm,' he said impatiently. 'Hold still.'

'I don't want to be warm—I want to be back at the theatre, doing my job.'

But even as she protested she was quick to push her fists
through the armholes of the coat in an attempt to preserve
a little of her modesty.

It was one thing to be onstage, where the audience saw
her at a remove, under rose-coloured trick lighting. Quite
another to have the man she fancied being treated to this intimate view of her body before he'd even taken her to dinner!

She had a very clear progression programme on this:
meet, date, and then, if everything appeared to be going
somewhere meaningful—get naked. She didn't reverse that
order.

Khaled had bulldozed through it in the space of twenty-
four hours and gone straight for the naked.

Although he was keeping his gaze manfully above her
chin-line, which was making her feel marginally better.

'I've had threats, Gigi—stupid, puerile threats—a follow-
on from all this press coverage about your cabaret slipping
into dangerous Russian hands.'

Those hands were currently distracting her by drawing
the sides of the coat together to cover her properly.

'You'll have noticed, *dushka*, that you're not the only person in Paris who doesn't trust me.'

She did actually trust him—she just wasn't very happy
with him at the moment. But she wasn't letting on, because
clearly give him an inch and he'd take—well, take her offstage in the middle of a performance!

He was securing a couple of buttons on the coat. She
could have done it herself, but neither of them seemed about
to acknowledge this.

'The media aren't giving me much choice about how to handle your safety.'

'My safety is none of your business,' she grumbled.

A shiver of reaction shook her and he gave her arms a rub, a little roughly, so that her teeth chattered.

'Stop manhandling me,' she snapped.

'You are cold,' he said, continuing to rub.

'And whose fault is *that*? Stop shaking me about! I'm not a chew toy for you to play with.'

He stopped rubbing. 'A what?'

She wasn't sure why she'd said that—only he'd gone all physical, and a bit of her was enjoying it, which wasn't right! 'Coco has one,' she mumbled, avoiding looking him in the eye. Then she ploughed on, 'Look, I won't go back onstage. Does that solve the problem?'

Gigi noticed that the lining of the coat still carried his body heat, and she was finding it unexpectedly comforting after her shock.

'This is a start,' he said, releasing her, and she could feel his gaze, dark and disturbing, on her skin. 'And now you're refraining from kicking me we can discuss this like rational human beings.'

'I *am* rational,' said Gigi promptly, pulling the folds of his coat up around her chin, teeth chattering, 'and if you'll take me home I would be most obliged.'

'Don't be naïve. Paparazzi are camped outside your flat.'

'My flat? How do you know that? How do they know my address?'

'You gave those people on the Champs-Élysées your name. I seem to remember you declaiming it like a town crier.'

Gigi instantly felt sick. He made it sound as if she was on the make.

She wasn't her father—always on the sell, always doing something for himself at the expense of other people. Including her. She tried always to do the opposite. All she'd wanted was to promote the theatre and build up their audience. She'd thought he understood that.

He cut through her muddled thoughts.

'You are going to need security for a few days.'

'I can't afford it.'

He looked at her as if she'd said something absurd. 'Naturally you will share my security.'

It was ridiculous, but she was sitting down and her legs still felt wobbly.

'How is *that* going to work?' As she spoke she drew her long wobbly legs up onto the seat and under her, so she was more securely covered, and noticed that he noticed them on their ascent.

She tucked the coat more modestly around her and his gaze cut to hers. She was surprised to see a bit of colour riding his cheekbones.

She'd been virtually naked in his arms and he'd covered her up like something in storage—but flash him some thigh and he zeroed in on it with all the subtlety of...well, a man.

Gigi wasn't sure how she felt about that, but she discovered she no longer felt so diminished.

'You will stay with me,' he said, as if there could be no question about it.

The tension in the car was changing from anger and confusion to something more charged.

Given her experience with men was more of the duck and weave variety, not the fly-to-the-Bahamas-with-me-baby, Gigi wasn't quite sure how to respond.

'Won't that just be playing up to this idea that we're in some kind of nasty beneficial relationship?'

She blushed as she said it.

'You're blushing,' he said, as if this were a wonder.

Gigi looked away. 'I am not. It's just hot in this coat.'

Which was when she noticed they seemed to have left the familiar *arrondissements*. There was less light and more lanes of traffic.

She tried to see out, but with the soft glow of light in the back of the SUV and the darkness outside she could really only see their reflections in the dark glass.

He was watching her as if she fascinated him. The feeling was mutual, but that didn't mean she was ready to go away with him. They hadn't even been on a *date*!

'I'm not going back to your hotel with you,' she said. 'My reputation may be shredded after today, but I'm not buttering it and putting jam on it.'

He gave her an arrested look. 'What is this jam?'

'Jam—you know, *jam*.'

'Sex,' he said coolly. 'No, I am not taking you back to the hotel.'

'Good.' Gigi tried not to let her disappointment show, because despite everything a part of her had leapt when she'd seen him striding across the stage towards her. Coming to collect her.

'We're going straight to the airport,' he informed her. 'I'm taking you with me out of the country—tonight.'

CHAPTER ELEVEN

S~~HE LOOKED LIKE~~ an angel. Her long, coppery red hair was snaking across the black leather of the seat, golden lashes lay recumbent on her high pointed cheekbones. Every last cinnamon-brown freckle stood out against the pallor of her scrubbed clean face. She had one slender hand cradling her cheek as she slept.

Against his better judgement Khaled reached across with one hand and lifted the blanket that had dropped from her shoulders to hang over her knees, and was now threatening to slide off completely. He draped it over her and returned to navigating the long stretch of highway taking them from the airport into central Moscow.

What the hell was he doing?

He'd been asking himself that question for the last three hours. The obvious answer was between his legs. The less obvious conclusion he'd come to was that he genuinely liked her. She might be a con artist and a stripper, but she had a way about her that had caught him unawares. And he could say this for her: he damn well wasn't bored.

Only now, when he looked at her sleeping, his suspicions seemed laboured and frankly untrue.

It was difficult to match up the wet, naked fantasy who had lied to him, furiously kicking her legs as he'd carried her offstage, with the soft-featured sleeping girl beside him, her face a study of the angelic, her impossibly long limbs curled up under her, her hair a swathe of burnished colour across the blue of the blanket.

A shower and a change of clothes had taken care of the gold-painted mess and the Gigi he'd spent the day with had been once more beside him. Khaled had been surprised by the level of his own satisfaction on that score.

He knew when she opened her eyes. He could feel them on him.

He glanced her way.

She blinked. Those eyes stayed on him. Very blue. She licked her lips. It should have been sexual. Instead what he felt was a warmth spreading through his chest.

She was safe. She was awake. He had no intention of letting her out of his sight.

It felt good.

She sat up, pushing back her fringe.

'Where are we?'

'Quarter of an hour outside Moscow.'

'What time is it?'

'Midnight. You lost three hours.'

'Where did I lose them?'

He tried not to smile. 'Back in Paris.'

'Along with my shoes,' she said. Then furrowed her brow at him. 'Why didn't you wake me up?'

'You were sound asleep—it was easier to carry you to the car.'

'You *carried* me?'

'It seemed the thing to do.'

She pulled on her sleeves, gave him an awkward sideward look. 'You've turned me into one of those showgirls who goes away with a wealthy man for the weekend.'

'Is that so?'

'I'm trying to work out how I feel about that.'

'Fill me in when you've decided.'

Gigi cast him another look. 'I guess I'm not here to sleep with you, so the nuts and bolts of that kind of thing don't apply, but nobody else knows that. It looks bad.'

It wasn't her imagination. He'd definitely tensed. Those capable hands, lightly sprinkled with dark hair at the broad wrists, flexed around the wheel and testosterone began to be pumped out into the atmosphere between them.

'Why do you care what other people think about you?'

'Twenty-two people, to be exact. The other dancers in the troupe. They already think... Well, never mind what they think. It's not true.'

Gigi thrust her hands into her lap and stared straight ahead. Khaled was silent. Apparently telling a man you weren't going to sleep with him after he'd gone out of his way to rescue you from a media scrum was a bit of a no-no.

Then it occurred to her that he might be tensing up because he had no intention of sleeping with her. In which case it made her sound desperate. Clearly she'd been on her own too long. She'd got cosy, living a charmed *Girls' Own* existence with Lulu, allowing her friend's anxieties about men to shelve her own fledgling sex life—until now, when you put her in the company of a gorgeous, testosterone-charged man and she began fantasising that he wanted her.

Gigi took another covert look at him. Most women would want him. He was built on a scale that made her think about that trip she'd taken to Florence, looking up at Michelangelo's *David*. Her attention dropped to the shift of his long, powerfully muscled thigh as he accelerated.

'I can hear you thinking,' he said, in that low, strongly accented voice, and Gigi jumped, her gaze yanked back to his.

Oh, God, he'd caught her looking at his groin. She wasn't doing that—honestly. She *wasn't* thinking about what she'd had pressed against her yesterday. Even if it *had* been memorable and she *had* been very flattered it had been to do with her...

Was she speaking this all out loud?

He glanced at her again. 'Don't worry, Gigi. I'm not listening in to your thoughts.'

Her face felt hot. 'It wouldn't matter if you were, I've got nothing to hide.'

'*Da*, I saw that onstage.'

Gigi straightened up. Reviewing her performance was fine by her. She could take criticism. 'I was on fire tonight,' she declared.

'Is that what you call it?'

She made a face. *Everyone's a critic.* 'Pity you had to spoil the act.'

'You were naked.'

Gigi bristled. 'I was not! I was in costume.'

'A piece of string.'

'Plus gold body paint and pasties. *And* shoes.' Her eyes narrowed. She wasn't going to forget what had happened to her shoes.

'That's not a costume—it's an incitement.'

'To what?'

He made a derisive sound. 'Are you serious?'

'Excuse me? I was *not* naked.'

'I saw *everything.*'

'You did not!'

'Maybe not everything,' he responded, and it was his turn to drop his gaze to *her* lap, 'but I saw enough.'

Flustered, Gigi crossed her legs. 'You saw what you wanted to see,' she snapped back, feeling ridiculously self-conscious. 'Lulu's right. Men have lurid and depraved imaginations.'

'Lurid and depraved?'

She could hear the disbelief in his voice and it had her sitting up straighter. 'You make things sexual that aren't.'

'You were swimming in a spotlit tank, on a stage, with two pythons wrapping themselves around your naked body,' he growled. 'How is *that* not sexual?'

She looked at him blankly. 'You mean Jack and Edna?'

'Who?'

'The snakes. Edna's an old softie. Jack's the one you've got to look out for—he can slap you around with that tail. Mind you, they're both way past retirement age, but Jacques wants to see this season out. The "Snakes in the Amazon" act is one of our most popular.'

'This would be because it's dangerous and because you are naked.'

Gigi smoothed her hands over the long, beautifully tailored pants he'd provided for her aboard the jet, entirely grateful that she wasn't virtually naked now. He was making it all sound grubby.

'Wow, you are *such* a prude,' she said uncomfortably. 'Who'd have thought it?'

'After your presentation, Gigi, I was under the impression that the place was a bit more classy. My mistake.'

What exactly was he implying? That *she* wasn't classy?

A hot feeling at his unjustified criticism shot through her, but what was sharper was the needling sensation that she had something to be ashamed of.

She didn't.

She did the best she could with the material she was given—act *and* costume. She should tell him there was nothing sexy about breath control underwater and managing two temperamental reptiles while keeping a big smile on your face for the patrons. It was hard work!

Besides, she wasn't keen on the pythons act herself, and she was fairly sure it was her complaints that meant Jacques would be phasing it out at the end of the season, but Khaled had no right to imply that there was anything tawdry about it or her participation in it.

She was already feeling humiliated enough after being trussed up and thrown over his shoulder like a naked turkey.

Better to say nothing.

She folded her arms. She really didn't want him to know just how utterly out of her depth she was feeling. The most excitement she ever got was pedalling a bicycle down the hills of Montmartre. She might play at being Gigi, Queen of the Amazon, onstage, but frankly she was Gigi, Queen of the Ordinary, in her everyday life. Tearing down a Moscow highway at midnight in a supercharged sports car with a man who dated supermodels wasn't exactly the usual end to a night onstage for her.

The problem was it seemed to be turning into one of those

episodes with her father, where she'd been forced to keep her opinions and fears to herself because he hadn't wanted to hear them—and even if he had it would just have been something he'd expected her to get over.

'You've grown soft, Gisele Valente,' she could hear him saying. *'Life's tough—you need to toughen up.'*

'Gigi?'

She sniffed.

Which was when something landed in her lap.

It was a phone. An elaborate little device.

'Eight-ten-thirty-three.'

'Pardon?'

'The international code to phone Paris. I thought you might want to ring someone,' he said gruffly. 'Your friends might be concerned.'

The fact that it hadn't even occurred to her until now startled Gigi.

Of course Lulu would be frantic! She hadn't been at the theatre tonight, but no doubt some of the other girls had spread the news of her being carried out in his arms.

Lulu probably had her stepfather pulling all kinds of strings at the Ministry of Foreign Affairs, where he pretty much ran the show.

She made the call. Lulu picked up immediately and shrieked her name, confirming her fears and forcing her to hold the device away from her ear.

It was even more awkward explaining herself with Khaled right beside her.

'I'm fine. He's not a murderer.'

She glanced at him, wondering what he was making of this, but Khaled's expression gave nothing away. She might have been talking about her shopping list.

'No, it's okay—I'll be back in a few days.' She turned towards the door and tried to keep her voice down. 'No, it's not a stunt. I'm in Moscow.'

'We're on Kashirskoe Shosse.' Khaled's deep voice cut

through the shrill sounds of disbelief in her other ear. 'Your friend can find it on a map.'

'Did you hear that, Lu? Yes, that's him. Yes, he is.' She lowered her voice. 'No, he hasn't.'

Khaled shifted beside her and Gigi wished the seat would swallow her up.

Lulu's description of the protesters' arrests and the media's interest was alarming. None of it had apparently been an over-exaggeration on Khaled's part. Then again, he had not yet struck her as a man given to anything but the stripped-down facts. It was something, given her murky past with her shyster father, she really liked about him.

Had liked about him…before he'd started going on about her act.

She listened as Lulu described how she'd had to wade through paparazzi to get into the apartment building and how she and Coco were staying with her parents tonight.

Khaled had told her the truth.

She glanced at him, feeling a little stupid for all the fuss she had made.

'People at the cabaret are talking about it like it's the romance of the century,' Lulu went on. 'I think some of the girls have even talked to the press.'

'Romance?' She said it out loud, before she could censor herself. 'I don't think——'

Khaled plucked the phone out of her hand. 'She'll talk to you tomorrow.'

Lulu must have said something cutting, because Khaled's expression was cool as he ended the call.

'She does not like me.'

What on earth had Lulu said?

'You might want to rein her in on making threats. They'll get her into trouble.'

Gigi blinked. 'It's *Lulu*,' she said faintly. 'She's not a threat to anyone.'

'Nor are you to feed stories to her while you are here.'

'Stories?'

'"Romance of the century..."' he drawled.

Gigi went hot. He'd heard Lulu's end of the conversation. He must have ears like a cat. A big, predatory cat—the kind who brought down the unwary.

She was beginning to feel distinctly savaged herself by this line of discussion.

'It's not me or Lulu—it's the other girls,' she defended herself.

'Who won't be receiving any bulletins from *you*, Gisele.'

'You can't possibly think I *want* people to be speculating about us—' She broke off awkwardly, not wanting him to think she thought there was an 'us'. 'I mean me.'

'Why wouldn't I think that? This is what you wanted, wasn't it? To revive interest in the cabaret? As I remember it you put together an entire presentation with that in mind.'

'For *you*,' she said, thrown by what he was intimating. 'I showed that to you—not the rest of Paris!'

She felt stupidly hurt, because she had been holding on to that interlude as one of the nicer interactions between them—something genuine, when she'd been allowed to show him what she could do. Weirdly, it had felt more personal than when he'd been expertly gliding her under him on the bed.

'You invited the rest of Paris in with that neat little speech on the Champs-Élysées.' He drummed the wheel with his fingers. 'Then there was your performance in the lobby of the Plaza.'

'I did *not* want to go up to your hotel room. You were the one who was so all-fire keen.'

For the first time it looked as if she'd scored a hit, because he didn't appear to have anything superior to say.

'You had an injury,' he said finally.

She'd had an...

Gigi pressed her lips together, aware that if she kept this up she was going to say something unwise.

Something that might see her standing at a bus stop at one in the morning on the side of a Moscow road.

Did they even *have* bus stops?

Light was smearing the windscreen and her gaze was drawn to neon advertisements, the glowing façades of sky-scrapers. The tension in her body increased.

This was the way she'd used to feel with her dad—that airless, suffocating feeling when she couldn't say the wrong word, do the wrong thing, because then she'd be out. On her own. Carlos's way or the highway. The only problem was she'd never quite been sure what the wrong thing *was*.

A feeling a little like panic began to spiral through her. It was bringing back her dependent teenage years with a thump. No say in where she went, what she did. *You're not powerless any more*, she reminded herself. *Those days are gone—you have options.*

She had her passport. She could take a taxi back to the airport. She could book a flight and have Lulu pay for it, using her credit card, and pay her back when she got home. She didn't *have* to stay with this man.

By the time they pulled up she had several speeches ready for him. But when she climbed out and looked up, took in the imposing building with caryatids on the stone columns either side of the entrance, and the doorman in uniform, she discovered her overriding feeling was one of nerves.

She wouldn't be intimidated. *She wouldn't.*

'Come.'

He took hold of her elbow none too gently and something inside Gigi tugged and tore.

She yanked her elbow out of his grasp. 'Stop being so horrible to me!'

'Horrible?' He stood over her, keeping the wind out of her face with those broad shoulders of his.

Gigi stepped a little closer, because it was cold, and he was big and warm, and even if he was being a horrible she trusted him.

'I want you to be nicer to me.'

'*Nicer* to you?'

He made it sound like a word in a foreign language, and maybe it was. Maybe she'd got this all wrong and she was just a nuisance in his world.

'I just think you could make an effort to be nicer to me,' she grumbled. 'After all, I've had a rough day too.'

He didn't respond, but he was looking down at her as if she had said something weird.

'Don't worry—forget about it.' She shrugged her shoulders and looked up at the building. 'Is this where I'm staying?'

He said something in Russian, but this time he didn't touch her or hurry her inside.

She tried not to feel self-conscious as she stood beside him in the lift taking them from the ground to the sixth floor.

She'd worked out that he wasn't very happy with her. She guessed she couldn't blame him. It wouldn't matter so much, but all the running about with him yesterday, the confidential talks, the amazing way he'd been with her insecurities over her feet, not to mention what had happened afterwards, had...well, had aroused feelings in her.

She didn't often have these feelings, and if she'd had a choice in the matter she wouldn't have picked him as the ideal target for them, but it wasn't as if she had any say in it. They were her *feelings*.

In contrast, Khaled didn't seem to think she had any—or was it just that he was so used to women falling into his lap?

She guessed he kissed women as if he was lost in the desert and the woman in question was water every day of the week.

It wasn't the same for her.

Before Khaled had taken her unawares on the bathroom vanity yesterday she actually hadn't kissed anyone since New Year's Eve—although that was something she'd be keeping to herself. He didn't need to know that her private life was the equivalent of a mill pond. She'd be holding on to her out-every-night-showgirl status, thank you very much.

Then the lift doors opened and she stepped out into what had to be the most glamorous lobby, fitted out in black and white marble and granite.

'Wow...' she breathed.

Movement-activated sensors shed low light through the hall ahead of them. It all looked very welcoming and expensive and intimate.

'Will I be staying *here*?'

He closed the doors behind them and his hand caught hers. Not a snatch, but a tangling of his clever fingers with hers.

Gigi's arm tingled. Her breath caught as he turned her around and she found herself looking up into beautiful dark eyes so thickly lashed it was a wonder he didn't need splints to keep the lids up. This inconsequential thought flew away with all the other butterfly thoughts about what she was doing here and why she felt so nervous.

She would never be too sure if she stepped towards him or he to her, only suddenly there was no space between them at all and she was in his arms.

This was her answer, she thought fleetingly, This was him being nice to her.

Very nice to her.

The need swelled up in her like a symphony as she lifted on her toes and wound her arms around his neck and held on.

She didn't know why, but when he kissed her she always felt as if she was on the deck of a ship. Everything was heaving up and down in the most delightful manner and she would lose her footing if she let go.

He re-angled the kiss, going deeper, moving against her, backing her against the wall. She moaned softly and kissed him back, her heart beating like a drum. She instinctively moved her hips, pressing her pelvis into his groin, feeling the length of him so impossibly hard against her.

At first all Gigi allowed in was a feeling of relief that finally the torturous suspension of this powerful feeling between them was over.

But then she discovered she couldn't shut down her thoughts, even though her body was going crazy with wanting him.

What was she *doing* here? Did she *really* think she could just give in to her feelings and forget about the consequences? She didn't even know what was in Khaled's mind. Would he think she was making up to him just for what he could do for her?

Stop thinking! she shouted at her busy little brain.

No. She couldn't give in to this physical longing, because that was all it was, when her motives must appear extremely ambiguous to him.

She broke the kiss.

It was the hardest thing to do in that moment.

'I don't want to be accused of using sex for leverage,' she panted.

'Ch'to?' His eyes were heavy-lidded and he was breathing hard.

'All the girls think I slept with you to further my career.'

'This is not a problem for me,' he responded, and his mouth moved over hers again, making it impossible to do anything but absorb the sensation, the fierce push of his lean, hard body against hers.

Still her mind kept beating, like the sea against a tethered boat. No...yes...oh, help. It was so unbearably exciting, and so unfair. He was being no help at all with her moral quandary! He branded her with that mouth of his and for a few incredibly exciting seconds she gave way.

It was even better than before because she just let herself *feel*. Her thighs literally felt as if a landslide was going on. She could barely hold herself up. But he was there, hard and powerful, doing all the supporting work a girl could need.

No, there was nothing to stop them...nothing but her conscience. Nosy, interfering thing that it was.

'Khaled?'

She wedged her elbows in between them to give herself some wiggle room.

'This can't happen,' she told him, even as she melted with pleasure over each hot, knicker-elastic-snapping kiss he laid down her neck.

If the other girls could see me now.

They'd kill her.

No, Susie would tell her to go for it—get that squeak fixed. Solange would scoff, because Gigi hadn't got a promise of *anything* out of him and she was just offering up the goods without a contract. Lulu would be horrified.

Forty-eight hours?

Gigi strained against him as he stroked a searching hand up under her sweater, under the completely unsexy thermal vest, and found a very happy to see him breast.

Oh, yes, her nipples remembered him.

Bad, *bad* nipples.

He circled one with the broad pad of his thumb and she whimpered, because she felt it directly between her legs.

He did it again and her knees buckled.

'This isn't fair…' she whimpered.

'Life isn't fair,' he responded against her mouth, as if he were telling her something she didn't already know.

The phone he'd gifted her began to vibrate in her hip pocket. At first it was difficult to tell, given that she was doing some serious vibrating herself in that area—but, no, it was a lozenge-shaped vibration, coming from the general vicinity of where she'd shoved the phone.

She broke the kiss and reached down between them. Khaled watched her actions as if riveted, and for a moment she wondered if he thought she was going in another direction.

No—she could have told him she wasn't that bold. She left that kind of forthright sexual move to girls with a lot more know-how than her. She was more of a wait-and-see what-he-wants-to-do-with-it kind of girl.

She held up the phone like a red flag.

'What are you doing?' he growled.

'Answering my phone,' she breathed, because he still had one hand cradling her breast. 'Excuse me.'

She pushed 'talk'.

'Hello, Lulu?'

Khaled stared at her as if she'd developed a second head, and as Lulu's voice complained at being hung up on she supposed she had. Khaled looked at the phone, and for a breathless moment Gigi wondered if he was going to smash it on the floor.

The part of her that had been anticipating that was to be severely disappointed.

He said something in Russian, his hand slid away from her, and she found herself on her own, slumped against the doorframe. Lulu was wanting to know if she was safe and telling her she didn't sound like herself.

'We've just arrived—barely got in the door,' she breathed, watching him stride away from her down the hall.

'You sound like you've been running a race,' Lulu countered suspiciously.

Gigi swallowed hard. 'No, no...just a flight of stairs.' It was only a little lie, and there was no way she was going into what had just happened. She wasn't even *sure* what had just happened. 'Look, Lu, I'm beat. I'll talk to you tomorrow. What time is it there?'

'Dawn,' said Lulu. 'I'm in bed with Coco, watching all the repeat coverage of what happened last night. They're saying Kitaev bought the cabaret so he could have you.'

'Have *me*?' Gigi knew she was red as a beetroot. 'I'm not a prop. And besides, he won the cabaret in a card game!'

'Maman says you have a pretty good case for slander.'

A court case? No, thanks.

Gigi began to make her way down the hall. Where had he gone?

Lulu was recounting several cases in which people had been defamed in the press and won huge payouts, but Gigi wasn't able to concentrate on a word. She needed to go in search of Khaled. Because right about now she was feeling she'd behaved like a rabbit, and she owed him an explanation—besides which, she didn't even have a bed to sleep in.

CHAPTER TWELVE

SHE PEERED AROUND the corner into one dark room, and then another. Honestly, it was a bit rude, leaving her on her own.

Which was when he appeared unexpectedly at the end of the hall, shirt unbuttoned.

'I'm not driving you back to the airport tonight.'

His deep, dark voice startled her, given she still had Lulu's high, melodious French accent in her other ear.

Gigi made her choice. She pushed 'end'.

'I think we should clear something up,' she said, trying to firm her voice.

'I agree. I know what you're going to say: I shouldn't have touched you.' He headed off around the corner.

Gigi almost broke into a sprint. No, no—that wasn't what she was going to say at all. 'Listen,' she said, following him down a flight of stairs, 'what I wanted to say was I know you're probably going to sell L'Oiseau Bleu.'

'Is that so?'

'Yes, and also everything that happened today is my fault and I'm willing to take it on the chin,' she said in a rush.

For such a big man he was incredibly light on his feet as he padded down the steps. He'd removed his shoes, and in jeans and an unbuttoned fresh shirt open across his chest he looked incredibly sexy, and for some reason younger, but also entirely beyond her reach.

'You didn't have to bring me here, but you did. And I guess you know something about press intrusion and I should be grateful—and I am. But I don't want you thinking I want something from you.'

Khaled stopped so suddenly she rammed into his back. Gigi was aware she'd been in this position before.

'Gigi,' he said patiently, turning around slowly, 'the only

eason we got into all of this was because you want something from me.'

'That's not true!'

She took a step back, because frankly she didn't trust herself within bumping distance of him. It took every ounce of her concentration to rip her eyes off his bare chest.

'Look, I know your cynical viewpoint was probably earned the hard way, but my life hasn't exactly been storybook either. I know well enough how mercenary and self-serving people can be, but that doesn't mean you have to abandon your best instincts. You've certainly spent enough time with me now to form some idea of my character and to know I'm not on the make.'

He shook his head. 'Gigi, at the moment I'm too achingly hard to laugh, but your indignation is rich, given the events of the last forty-eight hours.'

He was…? She tried to ignore the melting response of her body to the news that he still wanted her. God knew she wanted him. They just had things to discuss first.

Only he kept going down the stairs.

'I guess it suits you to think I want stuff from you!' she called after him. 'It means you can keep treating me like luggage and not talk to me about what happened between us in my flat and at the hotel.'

She shut her eyes briefly. She hadn't meant to say that.

'Why would I want to talk to you about it?'

'Oh, I don't know—because you kissed me?'

He looked up at her. The way his eyes ran over her body made her shiver.

'It was a mistake.'

Was it?

Which was when her stomach decided to yawn open and a noisy, unambiguous rumble made itself known.

Kill me now.

He frowned. 'When did you last eat?'

'Four o'clock. Yesterday.'

He said something clearly uncomplimentary in Russian

'What did you just say to me?'

'Stupid girl,' he said in English, but his tone was almos warm. 'Come on, I'll feed you.'

'Stupid being here with *you*,' she muttered. But she trotted after him.

He took her downstairs to the kitchen. He dug out fresh bread, ham, cheese, salad stuff, and went to work on sandwiches.

He did everything he could to get his mind off her soft-as-rose-petals lips, the pointy curve of her breast that fitted perfectly into the palm of his hand, her sweet enthusiasm even as she pushed him away and twittered nonsense at him about it not happening.

'You cook for yourself?'

He looked up. She was sliding her pretty little behind onto a stool at the bench, her blue eyes on him.

'Why not?' he growled, feeling like a bear with a sore head. Because she was right—it *shouldn't* happen. 'Every man should be self-sufficient.'

'Yeah, I'm getting that vibe off you.'

She fell quiet. He didn't trust her when she was quiet Gigi's mind didn't stop whirring.

'When I first saw you I thought, *Now there's a man who's* been *somewhere*,' she said suddenly.

'I *have* been somewhere. Central Asia and the Arctic Circle, with a band of scientists and geologists.'

'To do with your oil?'

She was a quick study—he'd give that to her.

'To do with my oil. There's nothing like being on the ground, seeing the erosion for yourself, experiencing it, watching the visible proof of changing migration patterns.

the changes to the soil. Stops me from getting comfortable or lazy about my responsibilities to the planet.'

'You sound like a bit of a green.'

Khaled shrugged. 'I grew up in the mountains—it's difficult not to be ecologically aware.'

'Do you miss it, now you're living in cities?'

'I head back into the mountains when I can. I also have shares in alternative energy source companies, and I'm moving away from petroleum.'

'What's it like, running the world?'

'Is that what I do?'

'All that money—do you ever count it? Or do you stop thinking about it at a certain point? I mean, I live from month to month, and my budget is always blown by week two.'

Khaled frowned. She was nervous—was that why she was talking so much nonsense?

He wasn't accustomed to sexual nervousness in a woman. The women in his life were bold, mostly self-serving, conscious of the desirability which they put such a value on.

Gigi's actions upstairs began to make a bit of sense to him.

'You need a good accountant, *dushka.*'

'I don't earn enough to warrant one. Not all of us own oil fields.'

'Money isn't always the answer, Gigi. I've got a project in the Caucasus Mountains facing local objection and I think a good deal of it is connected to my billions in the bank.'

'Why's that?'

He laid down the knife and leaned forward on his hands. 'I'm the local boy made good—it doesn't go down well there.'

'I just assumed you were from Moscow.'

'The first time I saw Moscow I was fresh out of the army and I'd washed up with a duffle bag and some ambition. Until then all I'd known was the mountains.'

Gigi settled her elbows on the bench, her chin in her hands, and fixed her beautiful blue eyes on him.

'Were you born there?'

'I was. My father was a career soldier stationed in Chechnya.'

He began piling the sandwich filling high, slapping thick crusty bread on top. His housekeeper was an angel.

'Isn't that a dangerous place?'

'My father took a bullet from a sniper when I was four,' he confirmed, eyeing her when she sat back, clearly perturbed. 'After that my mother struggled. She was forced back to her family in the mountains further west and remarried a sheep farmer. We never had any money—we just had sheep.'

'I'm sorry about your dad,' she said. 'It must have been awful for you and your mum.'

'Difficult for my mother. She was in her early twenties, had little education, and not much chance of supporting me on her own.'

'But she remarried?'

'He had land, a home—respect in the village. He rose to be head man. She believed it was better than what she'd had.'

'She had *you*,' said Gigi.

'She had a corner in her parents' home, where she was the disgraced daughter who'd married a Russian soldier.'

'Disgraced? Why?'

'She was pregnant before she married him—and where I come from, Gigi, Russian soldiers aren't exactly welcomed with open arms. There's a long history of guerrilla warfare in the mountains between Russia and the peoples of the Caucasus. Nobody was happy with their marriage.'

'Were your parents happy?'

Khaled suddenly became aware that he'd just told Gigi more about himself than he'd ever revealed—to anyone.

He didn't talk about this. *Ever.* He didn't need reminding of that part of his life. Why was it at the forefront of his

ind now? Probably because at the moment the building of
at road down south was swinging over him like an axe.

'How did we get on to this topic?'

His tone was one that had made grown men fall silent in
is presence. He hadn't meant to use it on her, but he couldn't
tem the tide of anger when it came to his parents.

Gigi blinked. 'I just wanted to find out a little about you.'

Yeah—her and a lot of busy journalists.

Then he remembered that photograph of her mother and
er own sentiments regarding her father. *He wasn't a reli-
ble man.* He guessed Gigi knew enough about broken fam-
lies for him to give her a little of what she wanted to hear.

'My parents loved one another very much.'

Gigi raised an eyebrow. 'You don't seem over the moon
bout it.'

'"Love" is a word that's used to cover a lot of ground,' he
eplied. 'I'm not a big fan.'

'I don't think we have too much say in who we love.'

He pulled a chilled jug of cold *chay* from the fridge.

'Love didn't save my father from a stray bullet, and it
idn't feed and clothe my mother, or shield her from criti-
ism when she was forced to come home. In fact love only
nade it a lot harder for her.'

'But how do you *know* that? Why couldn't it have been the
pposite? She'd known love and it was a wonderful memory
or her, something she might find again.'

The *chay* sloshed as he lifted the jug towards the bench.

'I'll tell you why, Gigi. My stepfather couldn't forgive her
or being in love with my father. It didn't matter what she
id—it was never enough to assuage his jealousy.' Khaled
anged the jug down with force. 'There was nothing won-
erful about the way he treated us.'

He realised he was breathing hard.

Gigi sat back, her brow pulled in that knot he remem-
ered from their first encounter, but she wasn't backing away
rom him.

'I think Carlos was in love with my mother even after sh refused to have him in her life. I'm sure that was why h came for me after she died. But it didn't translate into lov for *me*. He pretty much resented me from the start.'

'You were his blood—why would he resent you?'

'Because she loved me,' Gigi said, with devastating sim plicity, 'but she didn't love *him*.'

Khaled stilled.

'You see,' she said quietly, 'we have more in commor than either of us realised.'

His chest wall tightened. She was looking at him wit those bright, hopeful blue eyes and all he could think wa that it was like putting a little field hare in a cage with a gre wolf to compare their lives in any way. He could so easil tear her apart.

Gigi didn't seem to understand this. She didn't under stand who he was.

Right now he was relieved that he'd turned down the stair and not up—because if he took her to bed she was bound t read more into it than there was.

He would put her in a guest room tonight and a hotel to morrow. It was time to reassert the barriers between them

Instead he heard himself ask her gruffly, 'Your father i no longer in your life?'

'He's in Barcelona. We talk on the phone. I'm not goo at holding grudges. You don't seem to be either.'

He tried to ignore the fact that she was telegraphing some thing else with her eyes—something about what had hap pened upstairs. She was biting her lower lip.

'You'd be surprised,' he murmured. 'Tell me about you dad.'

She gave a rueful little shrug that held a great deal. 'H tries to make amends, but he's very old-school traditional— he thinks the way he raised me was right: being strict, with holding praise...'

'Winding cords around your young feet?'

'Oh, no, I did that myself, trying to please him. It was being lifted and lowered on the ropes every day that did it. Carlos is many things, but he's not a sadist.'

'Those marks on your feet make me want to meet your father in a quiet place,' he said with intent.

'It's not necessary.' She looked up at him through her lashes. 'Although the cavewoman in me appreciates the gesture.'

Shoving aside his very real desire to clear the table and haul her into his arms, he pushed a plate towards her and poured cold *chay* into glasses.

She needed food in her stomach—that was the only reason they were down here together—and then he would do the right thing and send her to bed alone.

If it killed him.

Gigi bit into her sandwich with gusto and moaned.

He was a dead man.

'Good, this is so good,' she mumbled. 'You're like the King of Sandwiches.'

'I'll mention that to my investors,' he murmured, watching her eat. 'You really *are* hungry.'

'This is normal for me. I eat like a horse. It's all the dancing.' She swiped at her mouth unselfconsciously.

Many women had gone to great lengths to seduce him. Not one of them had ever thought just to eat a sandwich.

He noticed he hadn't touched his own. Food wasn't a priority for him right now.

His skin felt tight, hot, and he couldn't help looking at the wondrous architecture of her dancer's body and the soft female curves of her breasts and bottom beneath her clothes. He'd had his hands on her, and he wasn't going to forget that any time soon.

To take his mind off it he concentrated on what she needed. He knew she must still be hungry and dug out some kirsch-flavoured dessert from the fridge.

While he was fossicking around Gigi was collecting the

two plates and wiping up where she'd splattered bits from
her sandwich. He paused with the fridge door open, taking
in the sight of Gigi pottering around his kitchen. Rinsing the
dishes. It all felt weirdly domestic.

He slammed the fridge door behind him.

'You don't have to do that,' he said, more harshly than
he'd meant it to sound.

She finished wiping the plates and gave him a self-conscious smile. 'I'm much messier at home.'

'But you're not at home.'

The smile faltered. 'No.'

Send her upstairs now. His conscience was drumming it
into him, but something primitive and a lot more persuasive
was rushing hot and insistent through his veins. Knocking
out the more civilised switches and allowing everything that
was natural and male in him to take over.

His resolve was gone.

She was so lovely, in every way, and he knew how the
night was going to unfold.

There would be no guest room.

'Come here. I've got something for you.'

Pink colour zoomed up into her cheeks, which told him
he wasn't the only one feeling this, but she approached him,
and Khaled was well aware that the hunter in him was re-
sponding to the fact she was a little skittish around him.

Her eyes fell on the bowl of dessert and then she lifted
them with an almost guilty expression on her face.

Sex and food.

How was he going to resist this?

Without even thinking about it, he spooned some straight
into Gigi's lips.

She held it in her mouth and her lashes drifted down as
she savoured it.

He felt it in his groin.

She swallowed.

He groaned silently.

'Feeling better?' he asked in a thickened voice, offering her another spoonful.

Those golden lashes came up. 'Yes.'

He cleared his throat. 'Still hungry?'

She nodded and reached for the spoon, but he held on to it. 'Let me.'

She licked her lips and a coil of heat thrummed in his belly. But there was nothing salacious about her actions— she was just enjoying her food. And strangely enough he was enjoying feeding her, looking after her, making her happy.

'No more.' She refused her sixth spoonful, shaking her head, all that heavy auburn hair tumbling forward to frame her narrow face.

Bozhe moy, she was lovely.

He was playing with fire.

She leaned forward unexpectedly and reached out, caught the sway of his silver chain and cross, tangled it around her fingers.

It reminded him of how she'd tangled her fingers in his chest hair to drag him into their first kiss. She was doing it again.

His libido growled.

'What's this?'

'My baptismal cross.' His voice had deepened with arousal but also with pride in something he hadn't always been proud of. 'I was christened Aleksandr, after my father and the saint in the Russian Orthodox Church.'

'Where did Khaled come from?'

'My mother. When she came back to the village she thought it was politic that I be known by the name of her father, and his father before him. It was the only name I knew after the age of four.'

Strange how after all this time it still weighed on him.

'I'm Catholic,' she said, tracing the cross. 'I don't have anything so beautiful.'

'I disagree.' He brushed the line of her jaw with his fingertips.

Her expression was a speaking look of welcome. It would have been easy to lean down and capture her mouth with his.

It had been his intention.

But upstairs he'd had an intention, and Gigi's little performance was still there in the forefront of his mind. If she needed seducing *he* shouldn't be messing with her.

Gigi knew before Khaled moved that he wasn't going to kiss her. She saw the decision in his eyes, in the way his jaw tightened, and although the air between them was thrumming she knew this man had a whole lot more self-control than she did—and if he'd made up his mind he wouldn't be changing it.

Her heart sank as he turned away and said something about showing her to her room.

Right. Okay.

She probably wouldn't see very much more of him after this. Tomorrow he would go back to being the guy in charge and she'd have to start thinking about her future, because the writing was on the wall.

Only right now they were alone together. His barriers were down and, although it might have been lack of sleep and all the excitement of the long day, she felt as if she might die a little if this was going to be it.

She already knew she was going to miss him when she went home, and that whatever happened with L'Oiseau Bleu she would never forget him. He was the sort of guy a girl would look back on a little wistfully and wonder *What if?* for ever.

Did it really matter at this late stage if she made the rumours true?

It was just between the two of them. It didn't have anything to do with the cabaret, or the other girls, or the Paris press. It was private—and couldn't what happened behind closed doors remain private?

Lulu had a hundred rules about men and dating, and all of them came down to the same thing. *Respect yourself.*

But Gigi rather thought the better thing was to be true to yourself.

It was the reason she'd climbed up on that tank two days ago, risking if not her limbs then her dignity. Despite that, she didn't regret it—and she wasn't going to regret this. Because sometimes a girl just had to do what a girl had to do...

CHAPTER THIRTEEN

THEY NEEDED TO SEPARATE.

Khaled reached into the fridge and grabbed a bottle of chilled water to take upstairs. He'd put Gigi in the guest room and book a flight home for her in a few days. He'd hardly have to see her.

'You'll probably be happier in a hotel,' he said, closing the fridge. 'I'm not going to be here and you might get lonely on your own.'

He turned around, bottle in hand, expecting her compliance.

Only Gigi was in the process of peeling her sweater off.

She was wearing a thin thermal vest underneath.

He'd wondered what that extra layer was upstairs.

No bra and visibly erect nipples.

That would account for why a thermal vest suddenly became the sexiest item of clothing he'd ever seen on a woman.

That was until she stripped it off and everything sensible stopped working inside his head.

Milky freckled skin…delicate, gracile build…and small, high breasts tipped with—surprise, surprise—cinnamon-pink nipples.

It crashed through him. He'd thought he'd seen her naked onstage. He'd seen *nothing*.

She'd been telling him the truth.

This was Gigi as she was. Not some kitsch cabaret fantasy of a woman, but real, warm, not entirely sure of herself and incredibly sexy because of it.

He wasn't an audience member, or even her boss. He was the man she'd chosen.

She gave him an uncertain smile. 'Do you want to get naked with me?'

Yes. Yes, he did.

It was as if everything that had come before had fallen away. There was just this.

And if this was Gigi seducing him it was working.

It was also entirely unnecessary, because the first time she'd looked up at him from her vantage point on the dusty floor of that stage he'd been hers.

'I take it that's a yes?' she said, and she closed the distance between them and began sliding his shirt down over his shoulders, not hurrying anything.

He felt the tips of her breasts brush against his chest and desire stabbed him as deeply as anything had in his life. He put his hands around her shoulders and felt the quiver through her delicate body.

Although she'd initiated this, he had the oddest feeling of having something not quite tame under his hands, and that any sudden move might change the trajectory of this encounter and see her scooting off into the underbrush—or running for her phone.

It was all beginning to make some sort of sense.

Her skin was like cool silk as he explored the narrow breadth of her back. Her whole body was trembling as she wound her arms around his neck, and now he felt the dancer's tensile strength in her grip, and when she looked into his eyes hers were bluer than blue.

'Khaled,' she said seriously, 'please don't stop now.'

'*Nyet*—no stopping,' he assured her, and lifted her in a single movement up onto the bench.

'Here?'

She blinked, and he wrenched his attention from her quivering breasts, alluringly close to eye level.

'Not here?'

'Maybe not…'

'Where? Anywhere you want.'

'You're a man—you're hardly going to argue with me right now.'

'This is true.'

Only he'd been arguing with himself since he'd set eyes on her, but right now he couldn't think of one damn reason why they shouldn't have this night.

He couldn't resist, and took one small cinnamon nipple into his mouth. She whimpered.

She tasted like heaven. She *was* heaven.

Her fingers tangled in his hair.

He used his tongue. He sucked. She made sounds of approval that invited him to move to her other breast and went wild against him.

Khaled knew he wasn't even going to get his jeans unbuttoned at this rate. He was going to disgrace himself like a fifteen-year-old boy with his first girl.

He had to slow this down. He wanted to take his time.

But he *had* to have her.

But not in the damn kitchen. Gigi deserved a bed.

He carried her up two flights of stairs and into his room. Khaled realised his mistake, but it was too late. Gigi was looking around his bedroom with a rapt look on her face.

'Holy Mary, it's the Arabian Nights.'

He'd forgotten the impression it made.

The keyhole doorway…the vast bed low to the ground… the gallery above where he kept his books. It had been copied from an etching of an old Muscovite *terem*. He supposed to a non-Russian it *did* look like an eastern fantasy.

For him it was an excellent use of space and the existing architecture.

He couldn't say she was the first woman he'd brought here, but she was one of only a few. This was his private realm, and he guarded that privacy, but his usual sense of needing to distract and create distance didn't come.

Gigi could sense a little tension in him as he lowered her feet to the floor. Her hair swung around her shoulders. He framed her face and kissed her. It was a deep, soul-stirring, come-and-let-me-show-you-things kind of kiss—the sort Gigi imagined she wasn't ever going to get enough of.

To her surprise he turned her in his arms and said her name against her throat—a rough whisper that shimmered down her spine as his hands skimmed over her unbearably sensitised breasts to curve round her jutting hips and spread across her belly, only to move up again and cup her breasts.

His breathing was gratifyingly heavy, his mouth hot against the back of her neck, and Gigi thought the backs of her knees weren't going to hold her.

'Khaled...?' She needed to say his name.

'*Vechno*—that's how long I've been waiting for you.'

'*Vechno*?' she breathed.

'For ever. I thought you were a hallucination,' he said into her hair, his voice rough as sandpaper. 'Tell me I'm not still in the desert.'

Her heart lifted.

'No—thank goodness! Imagine where the sand might go.'

Laughter rumbled in his chest, and it felt so good against her that she wanted to stay there for ever. Sparks and sensations were cascading through her like the most beautiful waterfall as he continued to circle her nipples with his thumbs, teasing them into points of unbearable sensitivity. He fondled her breasts and stroked her body as if touching her like this was all he wanted, and Gigi thought she might die of it.

But what a way to go.

She made a soft sound of relief as his mouth slid over the sensitive nape of her neck, and then she felt his kiss on the tip of her spine right down the centre of her to her molten core, where she simply combusted.

'Is this what you want, Gigi?'

She felt her heart spike at the thickly worded question, thrilled that he would still ask.

She turned in his arms and sought his mouth, and kissed him with all the sensuous passion he drew out of her.

This, this, this.

'Oh, yes,' she said against his mouth.

It was his turn to make a deep, gratified groan as he

cupped her bottom and brought her up against him. She wrapped her long legs around him and he feasted on her mouth.

He carried her over to the bed, lowering her onto her back. He knelt over her and undid the button at the top of her trousers, deftly rolled them down the length of her legs, taking his time to enjoy the milky, satin-smooth limbs he was uncovering, smoothing the way with his hands.

'Don't stop now,' she warned.

'*Dorogaya*, Hannibal's army couldn't stop me now.'

She was still wearing the tiny glittery G-string she'd worn onstage, and he ran his thumb under the string that held it around her hips, all the way to the heart-shaped piece of satin that preserved her modesty.

'This,' he said, 'is indecent.'

Gigi's breath hitched as he stroked beneath it, his thumb finding her clitoris all plump with need.

Kneeling over her, he looked as wild and untamed as he had when he'd come for her across the stage, his shoulders massively broad. Only this time he was stripped. His bare chest was covered in dark hair, arrowing down to an abdomen as taut as a drum and a deeply cut pelvis where the hair grew thicker.

Gigi's eyes were drawn to the thrust of his heavily erect penis. It was beautiful—like the rest of him.

She began to explore him with her hands, but Khaled was soon moving out of her reach, and any further attempts to pleasure him as he was pleasuring her exploded into a thousand inconsequential pieces as he snapped the string and bared her to his gaze.

She had a slender strip of golden-red curls. A lot of the girls had everything off—it was just easier, given their revealing costumes—but she'd wanted something to remind her she was a woman. Khaled seemed to appreciate it as he touched her there, his expression a little blurry with lust.

He slid down between her thighs, gently but inexorably

pushing them apart. He coaxed open the petals at the heart of her and found her hot and wet and very ready.

Gigi made a startled sound as he used the flat of his tongue to lap at her, and clutched at whatever she could get her hand on—the sheets, a pillow—tangling the fingers of her other hand in his thick hair. She felt shameless in her need as pleasure rocked her body like a little boat in a storm. She whimpered and keened, and when he lifted his head the boat was in pieces. She felt like a tiny piece of flotsam in the midst of a cyclonic tempest, poised for a moment on a high wave.

Through the blur of her own pleasure she saw muscle definition on him that she'd never seen on another man, and she couldn't help but run her hands over it, feeling those muscles contract under her touch.

He bent his head to her breasts, no longer tugging but feasting on her nipples until she could barely stand it.

'No more, Khaled,' she whimpered, yanking not gently on his hair. 'Please, I just want—'

He raised his head, those heavily lidded eyes and the most carnal of smiles sending her core body temperature through the roof.

'Just think about how achingly aroused I've been for forty-eight hours, Gigi. This is payback.'

Gigi tried to do the mathematical calculation, but it wasn't easy with her body on fire and with Khaled licking her nipples with the flat of his tongue like a big, wild cat.

He couldn't mean from the first time he saw her?

'But… '

'*Da*, you've worked it out—I'm *that* basic,' he growled, rising up over her and rolling on a condom with brutal efficiency.

The hard heat of him sinking into the wet heart of her was so welcome she almost wept. Maybe she did, because everything suddenly looked blurry.

He didn't rush, and he held himself still for her, waiting

for her muscles to relax and get used to the invasion, his eyes soldered on her expressive face.

Then he began to seduce her mouth with his and she melted around him, lifted her hips. He sank further.

'Oh…'

She could feel him so deep inside her. Too much.

He brushed the nub of her clitoris. Tiny nerves sang.

'Khaled…' she sobbed.

'That's my girl,' he crooned.

He drove into her and they both groaned. He built and built the gorgeous ache in her body and she met every stroke. They moved together, as if their bodies were made for this dance, and she knew she would die, she would just die, if she didn't reach that peak soon. And he took her there, holding himself in check with a gritted jaw as she pulsed around him.

Then he was moving again—harder, deeper. Her hands clutched at his shoulders as he licked her breasts and over she went again, gripping him, crying out. Thighs trembling, skin gilded with perspiration. This time he came with her, his deep groan speaking to her own bliss before he crushed her to the mattress.

Gigi wrapped her arms around him. *This* was what she needed—skin on skin, the weight of him anchoring her after the gorgeous devastation.

When he stirred she thought he would move away, but instead he took his weight on his forearms and his mouth sought hers so sweetly she felt astonishment. She clung.

His eyes met hers, heavy-lidded, still drugged with the pleasure they'd given one another.

Gigi rolled onto her side as he got up to dispose of the condom and watched him through her lashes.

She felt replete, but she wasn't sure what to expect next.

She simply didn't have the heart to say anything that might shatter what felt to her so intimate and new.

So she waited for him to say something as he came back to

the bed, lowered himself beside her. And then he did the most perfect thing—without a word he pulled her into his arms.

Gigi went to him. It was absolutely where she wanted to be.

Her heart was beating so fast.

She mustn't read too much into it.

This was animal warmth, she told herself. It was natural to cling together after their bodies had come to know each other so well, so fast. Natural to take what was on offer—body heat, a fleeting sense of security—to take comfort.

She closed her eyes and took the comfort. Told herself this elated feeling was merely part of the natural high after great sex. Told herself so many silly things. But in the end, with her cheek pressed against his shoulder, the warmth and solidity of him against her, she felt like staying there all night. Longer. Eternally.

Vechno. She knew the word now.

Khaled didn't say anything, merely grunted as if satisfied that he had her where she was.

It was the nicest sound in the world, she thought before sleep claimed her.

Well, she'd had her night with him. Now what?

Gigi eased her deliciously aching body into a sitting position, slid her long legs off the bed and, with a slightly *triste* glance backwards at Khaled's much larger, uninhibited body taking up most of the mattress, tiptoed off in the direction of the bathroom.

Under the bright lights she looked as if she'd been dropped head first into a spin-dryer. Her hair was sticking up, her eyes were sleepy, and she had a cockeyed smile on her face that just wouldn't go away.

She was also covered in the scent of him, and washing it off wasn't her first priority. She leaned into the mirror and eyed her reflection curiously.

'So, what exactly do you think you're doing, Gisele?' she asked aloud.

Apart from the obvious.

She giggled, and made a face at herself.

Her mouth was swollen, and she had beard rash in all kinds of places, but as she ran her fingers through her crazy hair she felt insanely good. There had been nothing awkward about last night, and although she could put that down to Khaled's experience, she rather thought there was something about the way they were together that just *worked*.

She'd never had casual sex before, so she couldn't compare it, but a deep female instinct told her that this wasn't how 'casual' felt.

She had never felt so connected to someone or so secure as she had in Khaled's arms.

It had her smile fading.

She'd grown up through her vulnerable teenage years with a father who'd put her through hoops—literally—to secure his attention. Nothing she'd ever done had pleased him. But it hadn't stopped her trying over and over, and she didn't need a psychologist to tell her that she feared sending herself down the same unsatisfactory path in an adult relationship with a man.

Which probably explained why she had never taken any of her previous romantic brushes with men very seriously. Better to be sure you wouldn't tumble into love when love, as far as she knew it, was akin to falling down a flight of stairs. However, she had *never* just tumbled into bed with a man after forty-eight hours.

She was frowning at herself, and at this development in her life, when Khaled appeared in the doorway, leaning there with that extraordinary muscular grace he'd applied so breathtakingly to making love to her. Naked, rubbing his chest as he yawned, he was looking incredibly gorgeous, with a lock of dark hair falling over his eyes.

Mine.

Gigi bit her lip. *No, not mine—borrowed.*

She tried not to cover herself. She had no problem with nudity—she'd lost a lot of her self-consciousness in those first months at L'Oiseau Bleu. You couldn't be too hung up about your body when you danced in the equivalent of a bikini every night. Still, it felt different with Khaled's gaze hot and heavy on her and her nipples visibly budding in the mirror.

No place to hide.

Given his penis was behaving the same way, she shouldn't be embarrassed.

Gigi dropped her chin and smiled as he came up behind her and put his arms around her shoulders.

'Do you do this a lot? Talk to yourself in the mirror?'

'Only when the person I want to talk to is passed out on the bed.'

He smiled then—a slow, incredibly sexy spread of his mouth in alignment with his dark eyes as they creased with appreciation.

'Last night was incredible,' he said against her ear, sincerely, kissing her neck, lifting his face so that his dark gaze met hers in the reflection.

They looked good together. Complemented one another. Him so dark and male, her so tawny and female, her lithe frame bracketed by his powerful body.

Gigi even thought she looked a little beautiful this morning, as if all the happy exercise had given her a glow.

Which didn't explain the glow inside her.

She felt as if she'd swallowed sunshine.

'But, Gigi...' he said, and he looked very serious. 'I'm not a good bet if you're looking for any more than this.'

Gigi had the quick wits to respond before hurt got a hold. 'Why is it men never say those words *before* sex—only afterwards?'

Colour actually scored his high cheekbones and Gigi, despite the way her stomach was hollowing out, almost smiled.

What worked in his favour, aside from his obvious discomfort, was the fact that he kept his arms around her—as if he had no intention of letting her go.

Still, it was a bit rich, his assuming she would have 'catch and contain' plans for him. She had a very nice life, thank you very much, and she didn't intend to swap it for hot nights in Moscow with him.

So she let him have it. 'I should probably let you know I've got a ten-kilometre rule. I only date men who live within ten kilometres of Montmartre, otherwise it just gets too difficult. If it got serious he might want me to move, and I won't be doing that.' She raised a brow. 'So *I'm* not a good bet if you're looking for any more than this.'

Khaled lifted his head away from hers. 'Ten kilometres?'

'Don't worry,' she said with a little smile, 'we'll just consider this a weekend fling—that way we have the back-to-the-real-world clause open to us. You can go back to your normal, and I'll go back to mine. Deal?'

Khaled's arms tightened around her and there was a frown in his eyes. 'This is what you want?'

Gigi didn't have a clue what she wanted. She knew what she *liked*. She liked his arms around her, the closeness physical intimacy had brought them, but she already knew this was probably the biggest mistake of her life.

If she let it be.

She wasn't going to do that.

But her fighting words were already beginning to topple because he might be saying one thing but his body surrounding hers was saying another—and she was fairly susceptible to his body.

She'd have to watch out for those mixed signals. She didn't want to get confused. She really didn't want to find herself jumping through hoops to make him pay attention to her. She'd been there, got the T-shirt.

No, she needed to hold on to her independence even if it

choked her. She was perfectly capable of meeting his sophistication with some of her own. Yes, she'd definitely do that.

She lifted her chin. 'Sure.'

He let her go. Only to slide his hands over her hips and delve down between her thighs. Heat followed those hands and Gigi arched her body helplessly back against him.

He cupped one breast and plucked at her nipple as his other hand teased and pleasured her. She turned her head to try and kiss him but he was controlling their movements, and when he gruffly told her to put her hands forward on the bench she did as she was told and he entered her.

The eroticism of the movement took her unawares, and then he was moving inside her, guiding her hips with his big hands, and she couldn't think—only feel. Her body had become a vessel for their mutual pleasure, until she splintered into a thousand pieces and he followed her.

Gigi turned, clumsy and off-centre, not sure what had just happened, wanting connection and touch and to be kissed.

Khaled curved his hand around her cheek and she strained upwards to kiss him. For a moment she thought he was holding back, but something flashed in the back of his eyes and with a groan he lowered his head and kissed her with all the lush romanticism she could have wished for.

Then he scooped her up and carried her back to bed and began all over again.

CHAPTER FOURTEEN

'HAVE YOU GONE *LOCO*?'

Khaled pictured the long-legged, red-haired beauty he'd left less than an hour ago, sleeping like a Burne-Jones pre-Raphaelite maiden wrapped in white sheets, and thought maybe he had.

This raging possessive feeling inside him *was* a form of madness.

Which was why he'd needed to go for a run. Clear his head. Get some space between him and the woman he'd left in his bed.

Now he was loping back through the park across the road from his apartment building, his phone against his ear, his old friend's amusement putting some perspective back into the picture.

Alejandro du Crozier had experienced his own share of media attention. He was one of the world's highest-paid polo players, and the paparazzi had a love affair with the Argentinian's private life.

'The press are calling it a kidnapping. I hope she's worth it, my friend.'

Khaled frowned. He wasn't discussing Gigi. Even if her actions *had* brought much of this upon herself, the woman he'd come to know did not deserve to be the target of spurious stories in the media. And after last night he didn't want to discuss her even with Alejandro, and they had shared a lot over the years.

The Argentinian had rolled up in the gorge below Mount Elbrus several years ago, looking for Kabardian breeding stock, and a business relationship had turned into a strong friendship. Khaled was not a man who had many friends, but he took those he had seriously.

Still, he would not discuss Gigi with him.

She would be distressed to know he was even talking about her.

She wasn't as sturdy as she tried to appear. There was a gentleness inside her that brought out instincts in him he had made a life's work of repressing.

The fact that he knew this about her wasn't what bothered him. It was that he cared.

She didn't guard herself or put on a pretence of sophistication—she was simply herself.

Which was when it struck him that she couldn't possibly have been a knowing participant in her father's petty crimes. If he'd ever really believed it.

She had a redoubtable quality in her that probably made her a good and loyal friend, and that explained why her little flatmate had been ringing the phone off the hook—she was clearly concerned for her well-being.

Khaled wasn't unaware that if something happened to him the only people to weep and wail would be his shareholders.

He liked it that way. He didn't want people feeling responsible for him.

His mother had given up any chance of a real life to make sure he was raised in her home village. He hated that knowledge. It had haunted him all his life. So he'd been careful not to form relationships where sacrifice was involved. Of any kind.

He was generous in his sexual relationships with women. He made sure the women concerned were happy, and usually his money took care of that. Just as he was using his wealth and his influence to shield Gigi from the media. But emotionally he didn't risk anything—which was why his unease about Gigi was like taking a step into the dark.

Shaking it off, he turned the conversation back to sport and to horse stock before he finished his call with Alejandro and headed across the road. He was anticipating finding Gigi awake and dressed and off-limits.

He was just going upstairs when a call showed up from his

lawyer in Nalchik. He tore his attention away from a mental image of Gigi naked, with that little half-moon smile tilting her expressive mouth.

'They want to talk.'

Everything but Gigi's little smile fell away as he stopped in his tracks, unable to credit what he'd just heard.

'Talk next year or talk in the foreseeable future?'

'Tomorrow.'

Even as he listened to his lawyer lay it all out he called up the internet sites of Moscow's major papers. It was all there

Kitaev conducts Tartar raid on Bluebird in Paris.
Bride-stealing gets an update as Russian oligarch
plucks his bird of paradise.

'The elders believe you've shown respect for tradition. It seems they believe the "romance of the century" story. It's done the trick.'

Two years.

Two years and *this* was what shifted the balance?

Khaled didn't know whether to laugh or curse.

'I'll fly down tonight.'

'Not just you,' said his lawyer. 'You need to bring this woman.'

For a moment something sharp and hot and entirely violent passed through him.

'*This woman,*' he growled, 'has a name.'

'Miss Valente.' He literally heard his lawyer swallow. 'It is advisable, given she appears to have swung the vote.'

Which meant, effectively, that Gigi wasn't going home. Not yet.

Khaled exhaled, shoved his phone into his back pocket and strode energetically down the hall, pushing open the door, struck by how good he felt. He put it down to finally getting his hands on the road.

Gigi wasn't in bed. She was sitting on its edge, rolling a

pair of tights up her legs. Her incredibly long, dance-honed legs. His eyes followed all the way up to a pair of white cotton panties that somehow did more for him than last night's teeny-tiny bit of gold dental floss.

She looked up as the door reverberated on its hinges.

He whipped his T-shirt up over his head, tugged his sweats and briefs down and powered her back onto the mattress.

'Khaled!' she shrieked, giggling.

'Gigi.'

He fastened his mouth to hers and her body leapt under his. He dragged her top up over her head and her hair sprayed everywhere.

'Do you *ever* wear a bra?' he groaned, as if it were a complaint—or a prayer.

Gigi parted her lips to speak but his mouth was there first, and then he began to make love to her until she was wrapping her long legs with those dangling tights around him, making happy cries.

She was still panting when he collapsed and buried his face in her lovely silky hair, inhaled the scent of her. He could do it all over again.

But he'd had a purpose before he'd been distracted.

He sat up and looked around.

Gigi watched him with slightly glazed eyes. Waking up alone had not been the best of feelings, but she'd tried to be pragmatic about it, given their conversation in the bathroom. This pragmatism was going to be a little hard to hold on to if Khaled insisted on doing *this* to her every time the mood struck him.

To her astonishment he vaulted over her and began rummaging in the bedside drawer.

More condoms? Again?

Gigi was a little amazed to discover that her blissfully aching body was on board with that.

But after a few moments he wrenched the drawer loose and emptied it onto the bed.

She sat up. 'What on earth are you doing?'

'I'm looking for your passport.'

Gigi went cold.

She didn't think—she acted. She grabbed a pillow and whacked him hard across the back with it.

It was like using a feather to swat a water buffalo. 'Hey,' he said, giving her an almost boyishly baffled grin, 'what's that for?'

'Timing!' she hurled at him, and leapt off the bed and marched into the bathroom, slamming shut the door. Then throwing the lock for good measure.

He thumped on the door.

'Not. Coming. Out.'

'Gigi…'

He didn't sound angry. He didn't even try the lock. She waited a few minutes. Nothing.

Cautiously she opened the door and found him throwing clothes into an overnight bag.

She picked up her new grey trousers, which he'd left in a puddle on the floor last night, and threw them at him. *Hard.* 'Check the pockets.'

He retrieved her passport and tossed it to her. 'There'll be a border check—you'll need this.'

Gigi just stood there, her heart pounding. *He wasn't sending her home?*

'You'll need to pack a bag, Gigi.'

She folded her arms. 'I didn't agree to go anywhere further than this with you. Khaled, I have to go home—my job's at stake.'

'Your job's fine. I'm the boss, remember?'

'For how long?' She hadn't meant to ask, but now they were having this conversation she intended to find out.

'Long enough for you to pack a bag and come with me now. Listen, I'll look after it for you—you don't need to worry about your job, *malenki*. Come with me now, and when we get back we'll work something out.'

'Don't *do* that,' she blurted out. 'Don't make out that I'm with you because of what you can do for me. I've not asked you for one thing to do with the cabaret since we left Paris. That's not what this is about. I won't let you make it into something it's not.'

Khaled stilled. 'What is it, then, Gigi?'

'Great sex,' she whispered, her chest hurting. 'I thought that was what we'd agreed—you can't change the rules now.'

She waited for him to say that he hadn't, that he wasn't looking any further ahead, that he didn't want to try for something a little more committed. Then *she* would say, well, she didn't want that, she was quite happy with what they had. Only maybe one night was enough—because she wasn't sure her heart could survive any more nights and days knowing there was no future between them.

But she wouldn't say the last part, because it made her sound like an unsophisticated ninny.

'So I am no longer great sex?' His tone was surprisingly gentle.

Her heart lurched, because he was trying to make her smile, trying to wind this back a notch. And that was a relief—because they were entering territory it was probably best they didn't.

'Well, you *are*…'

He didn't mean for you to answer, eejit, he meant it rhetorically.

'But I guess you know you are.' She frowned. She was stuffing this up. 'What I mean to say is that I didn't mean to reduce you to something physical. I mean, it's not like I'm out there every night with men drinking champagne from my shoes or something.'

Way to go—impress him with your showgirl lifestyle, Gisele. Tell him about your knitting project—that'll put an end to this.

'You surprise me,' he said, in that dangerously quiet way of his that made her think he might be laughing at her again. Only when she took a peek he looked a million miles away from laughing.

It suddenly occurred to her.

'You don't want me to go? Home, I mean?'

He said something soft and exasperated in Russian and she stayed where she was as he walked up to her, took her face between his hands and looked at her.

Really looked at her.

Gigi got lost in his dark eyes.

'Gigi, I've got to go south for business.'

Then he kissed her. And although she'd thought he had already kissed her and she had kissed him last night in all the ways imaginable, this was so lushly romantic, with his hands in her hair, and her hands curled trustingly between them, it felt new. It felt like the first time. Not just between them, but like her first kiss.

Gigi opened her eyes to find him gazing down at her, as if the kiss had astonished him too.

'My mother's people are indigenous to the region of Kabardino-Balkaria in the mountains of the North Caucasus.'

He spoke with a quiet sincerity that moved through her like a promise.

'I tell you this because I have a place down there, at the foot of Mount Elbrus. We can be alone for a couple of days. No work, no interruptions...' he gave her a smile '...great sex.'

Then he sobered.

'I want to show you where I come from. What matters to me. Give me that time.'

More time to stumble deeper into this. To lose a little more of her ability to find her way out.

His next words didn't make her heart lift as they should.

'Then I promise to return you to Paris.'

* * *

He hadn't told her it would be like this.

Gigi lay in a cot of marmot fur in Khaled's strong arms and watched the moon and stars through their own private observatory.

'Why did people stare at me in the village today?'

'You're the exotic creature I've snared in my net. If I'd hunted and skinned you they couldn't have been more surprised.'

Gigi frowned. 'Because of what was printed in the Moscow papers about me being a showgirl? I guess this is a pretty conservative place.' She raised her head to look at him anxiously. 'It won't get you into trouble, will it?'

He was quiet, and then he said in that low, sleep-gravelled voice Gigi liked to pretend no other woman in the world had ever been privy to and belonged only to her, 'Other men may try to lure you away…that's about the extent of it.'

'If they use cake I can't promise not to go.'

'That's my girl.'

She looked up archly. 'I think you could have left me in Paris.'

'Do you?'

'Yes, I do. I don't think I was in much danger at all. I think it's perfectly clear you wanted an excuse to act like a Russian he-man—'

This earned her a squeeze around her waist.

'—to sling me over your shoulder like a kill and bring me with you without the chance that I might turn you down!'

Khaled put his mouth to the shell of her ear. 'You've found me out.'

Gigi beamed.

It had been this way since they'd left Moscow and flown into Nalchik two days ago, and then driven for miles along a highway that could be described at best as bumpy in a landscape that had taken her breath away.

Deep valleys, high mountains peaked with snow… At

one point huge mountain deer had forced them to a stop as they crossed the road.

He'd brought her in the gathering dusk to a gorge littered with tall stone fortresses. Khaled had told her he'd refurbished this one, all six storeys of it, and they were now on the top floor, with its glass ceiling and panoramic views.

He had tossed her into this cot filled with marmot furs, pulling off her clothes and some of his own like a man possessed, and had made love to her with such fierceness and tenderness Gigi couldn't help feeling a little way in over her head.

After all, he'd made this amazing romantic gesture—bringing her here.

'I've never brought a woman here before.'

Okay. He had her attention.

'Why is that?' She tried to sound casual.

'Hmm?'

She frowned at him and wondered if she acted like one of those female mountain goats they'd seen yesterday trying to get a male's attention, bucking and sending clods of earth into the air so he'd get the message.

'Why have you never brought a girlfriend here?'

'I haven't had one to bring.'

She rolled her eyes. 'Right. So what was Alexandra Dashkova?'

'Who?'

'She had herself wrapped in a rug and rolled out before you.'

'Did she?'

'The other dancers were talking about her,' Gigi persisted, because *Didn't she?* wasn't going to cut it.

'I've met her several times socially—we've never been intimate.'

Gigi didn't know why, but something very heavy that she hadn't even known was pressing down on her chest suddenly wasn't there any more.

'I guess people write all sorts of nonsense about you. I should know.'

'Some of the nonsense I don't mind. The truth is none of the women I've been involved with are the kind of people I'd bring here.'

There was a lot to unpack there, so Gigi went with, 'Too glamorous?'

He grunted noncommittally, which made Gigi think she'd got it right.

'So I'm the mountaineering kind?'

'You don't strike me as particularly outdoorsy, Gigi.'

'Oh, I am. I've just never climbed a mountain before.'

'There's a first time for everything.'

CHAPTER FIFTEEN

HE SHOWED HER waterfalls where the water was crystalline and made love to her in a hot stream where the mineral were said to cure everything from aches and pains to old age—neither of which were on Gigi's mind as her wet, naked body cleaved to his against a slippery boulder, where they were afforded the smallest privacy from anyone else trekking in the area.

They climbed high enough to find wild mountain goats grazing on meadow grass and he told her about his youth working as a shepherd with his stepfather's flock. About his dog, his knife and the wild animals he'd encountered.

He told her about the threat from poachers who had nearly wiped out the entire mountain bison population here. He took her up to the top of Mount Elbrus by chopper and pointed out the area where his company was putting in a resort using prefabricated eco-friendly modules from Denmark.

'The more eco-tourism we encourage into the region the further we can push the poachers out.'

Gigi understood his commitment to the natural world. How he kept it in tandem with the oil holdings that had made his fortune. And it made sense that he was diversifying as he moved further away from an industry known to be aggressive against the planet. How could you grow up in this place and *not* care about keeping it alive?

She knew now that he was an extraordinary man— nothing like the one-dimensional, showgirl-eating beast the whole of Paris believed was going to devour their candy-coloured theatre. He was her lover, and she thought her friend, and really she'd do better with the latter.

Maybe when this was all over she could keep him as a friend.

But that wasn't likely, was it? Her pain when this was

over was going to be intense. They were sexually involved now and there was no going back from that.

Nobody lived in that world.

Nor would she want to.

They headed for the truck. It was the middle of the afternoon and everything was bathed in sparkling sunlight.

It was difficult to believe this had ever been a place of darkness for Khaled.

But it had, and she didn't want to ignore that. *He* hadn't ignored her poor, damaged feet.

She angled a look up at his beautiful broad features. 'How old were you when you left here?'

He stopped, and the look on his face had her heart pounding like a drum. He looked…surprised, then thoughtful. She'd expected him to clam up.

'Do you remember the highway we came in on? When I was fifteen I filled a duffel bag and hiked up it all the way to Nalchik.'

'For a job?'

'You could say that. I was working for the local crime boss.'

'Oh,' said Gigi.

'Welcome to twenty-first century Russia, *malenki*.'

'I take it you did well out of it?'

'Well enough to start selling black market imports at a local market.'

'I guess you did well out of that too?'

'Enough to invest with a friend in a company. Then I did national service. After that I made the move to Moscow.'

He folded his arms, his sleeves rolled up to the elbows. He looked so inherently masculine as he surveyed the valley around them that he took her breath away.

'It doesn't say any of this on the internet.'

He gave her a bemused look, but there was affection in it. 'I don't broadcast it, Gisele.'

No, but he'd told *her*.

'Why did you leave when you were fifteen, Khaled, when you clearly have this place in your blood?'

The remnants of his smile reconfigured into something she had seen in his face before when he talked about his past but hadn't understood.

'I would have killed him if I'd stayed.'

'Your stepfather?'

'I was big enough then—and angry enough. I also had the skill. There was just the two of us. He taught me how to track and make a clean kill, and how to cover my traces.'

Gigi said nothing, because now she understood.

'He taught me everything I knew at that age about being a man—and that's the catch. He was a man without honour, and yet he taught me our code the same way the army taught me how to assemble and disassemble a rifle in the dark—and because of that he got to live a little longer before liver cancer dragged him off, and I got to live with the question I ask myself every day. Did I make the right choice?'

'Of course you did.' Gigi turned up her face, wet with tears. 'You were just a child. You did the right thing and you survived.'

'I haven't shocked you?' he asked, and she could see the strain behind his eyes.

He cared what she thought of him.

'The only thing in that story that shocks me is how you became this man. This good, kind, decent man.'

He blinked, as if her words made no sense to him.

'I've never seen you cry,' he said, as if this were the wonder, and not the fact that he'd survived as he had.

'I only cry when there's something to cry about,' she said, wiping at her eyes.

He took her face between his hands and kissed her. Sweetly at first, then fiercely, and then they just stood wrapped around each other by the truck.

He stroked her hair. 'What am I going to do with you, Gisele?'

'I don't know,' she murmured against his neck, aware that e'd probably told her much more than he'd meant to over le last few days and later would be uncomfortable about it nd withdraw back into that place where she couldn't fol- w him. But right now she had him out here in the sunlight nd she was going to do what she could to keep him there.

She looked up and gave his beard a gentle tug. 'I do think 's time to take this off.'

But even as she spoke her phone vibrated in her back ocket.

'Your friend is doing me a favour,' said Khaled as she ook it out.

Sure enough, it was a text from Lulu.

It had been sent yesterday, but the WiFi in the tower was poradic at best.

Dantons out. Theatre shut. Thought you should know.

For a moment Gigi did nothing. Then Khaled's hand losed over hers and he took the phone. He didn't even look t the message. He just looked into her eyes.

She stumbled back.

'Why did you fire the Dantons as managers?

Khaled rested his hands on his lean hips. 'The Dantons ouldn't manage their way out of a paper bag.'

'That's it? That's all you've got to say?'

He shrugged.

Gigi shook her head, utterly confused by his refusal to see this as important. Didn't he care about her feelings at all?

He was watching her closely, and bizarrely Gigi won- dered if this was a test.

'I have shut the theatre down for renovations, not for sale. This is what you wanted.'

The wind in the trees was the only sound.

Gigi ventured a little closer. 'You're not selling?'

'I have heard nothing but how important this place is t you—why would I sell?'

Gigi put her hands against her sides, because there wa a sudden feeling like a stitch under her ribs.

'It will reopen in six months. I want you to manage it.'

'What?'

'You heard me.'

The stitch stabbed at her. She was suddenly utterly ter rified. She turned and wrenched open the truck door an climbed inside, slamming it shut after her.

In the warm quiet of the cabin she tried to make sense o what had just happened.

Khaled took his time coming round, swinging his large frame inside. He wound down a window, propped an elbov on the ledge and said, so reasonably and so authoritativel\` that she could only stare at him, 'You've got the passion the vision—you've even got the skills. With the right peopl\` behind you I can't see why you won't make a success of it

'What skills? I'm a *dancer*, Khaled, I'm not a business woman. I thought that would have been obvious when turned up at your hotel like a crazed stalker and chased yo\` through the streets of Paris and thrust a laptop at you.'

'Imagination, guts, determination. *I'd* hire you, Gigi, i\` we weren't in a relationship.'

'You *are* hiring me!' Gigi's whirling thought processe ground to a halt. *Hang on. Rewind.* 'Did you just say we're in a relationship?'

'It makes things—what was your word?—*murky*. I smacks a bit of nepotism, and I know you're touchy abou that.' He drummed his left hand on the window frame, look ing out across the gorge below. 'But sometimes, Gigi, grea things grow out of the most unlikely seeds.'

Gigi was busily sorting through everything he was throw ing at her. It was a bit like being tied to a circular board—a\` she had been as a fourteen-year-old—and being spun whil\`

someone threw knives at her. Only some of the knives had turned into bouquets of flowers.

'But what if I fail?'

'I'll replace you.' His dark eyes settled on her now and his expression was serious. 'This is a genuine business decision, Gigi. It has nothing to do with how beautiful you are, or how incredible you are in bed.'

Was she? Beautiful? Incredible in bed?

'This is all about what you showed me on that first day. Best job interview I've taken.'

'What usually happens in your job interviews?' she asked unnecessarily.

'I grill people.'

'You didn't grill *me.*'

'What do you think that run down the Champs-Élysées was about?'

'Now you're funning me.'

'The bathroom vanity was all about the fringe benefits, and back at your place I was checking out the facilities.'

Gigi wanted to laugh, but she also felt sick—because he didn't know the one thing about her that made all of this impossible.

He'd find out soon enough—someone would object to her elevation and then all the old stories would emerge. It wouldn't take much digging at all.

Carlos Valente, small-time con artist and his dancing daughter.

She didn't know what was on the internet—she'd never wanted to look. But she could guess that there would be some record from past English newspapers.

She'd been lucky it hadn't come up in the current coverage of 'The Showgirl and the Oligarch'. She guessed the main thing exercising people's minds was her showgirl feathers tickling Khaled's chin…and other parts. The story of a teenage girl travelling round England's provincial theatres several years ago with her sleight-of-hand father was less sensational than a sex scandal with a rich man.

It *would*, however, be of interest to Khaled when he discovered the truth.

He would look at her differently.

He would know of her less than savoury background and he would judge her.

And she couldn't blame him.

You couldn't let someone like *her* undertake this kind of job.

It was a position of trust. The first thing that went wrong and the finger of blame would be pointed at her.

Gigi panicked. Her heart went into overdrive.

She wanted out of this car.

Only even as she looked at the door handle she knew she wasn't going to run from this.

'Khaled, there's something you need to know.'

She clutched her hands together in her lap and began in a low voice to tell him about her father, his petty thefts up and down the country, and how it had all caught up with him one night in a Soho nightclub.

Khaled said nothing and allowed her to spill it all out.

She told him how she'd been arrested, put in a cell, interviewed, bailed. She told him about being acquitted nine months later, and that her father had been given a suspended sentence.

She told him how one of the reasons she'd gone to Paris was because no English club or theatre owner would employ her.

'I like the other story better—about my mum being a showgirl.' She bit her lip. 'But it didn't really start out that way. I don't know if I ever would have had the guts to try out for the Bluebirds if it hadn't been impossible for me to get a job in London. Not even Lulu knows the real story. I'm not really as brave as you seem to think I am.'

Khaled was looking out across the gorge, his profile un-readable.

'I won't make a fuss if you've changed your mind now,' she said huskily, her tongue sticking to the top of her mouth.

In response Khaled started the engine.

'I won't be changing my mind,' he said.

Gigi released a huge, shaky breath.

'Do you trust me?'

'A woman who has a blade poised at my carotid artery? Why not live a little dangerously?'

Gigi gave a nervous laugh, but she was sincerely worried about this first stroke of the blade. Trust Khaled to insist that an electric version wouldn't do the job and produce this cutthroat razor. After they'd returned from the mountain he'd stropped it for her and spent half an hour taking her through the procedure.

They nestled in the grassland that lay beyond the tower, Khaled perched on a fisherman's stool and Gigi standing with a towel over her shoulder, a bucket of warm water and the cutthroat razor in hand.

'You've never shaved a man before?' he queried as she practised using the blade on a small section of her forearm, where fluffy golden hairs grew.

'The opportunity has never arisen.'

She'd never actually lived with a man, and her former boyfriend had used an electric razor as far as she knew. Frankly, none of the boys she'd dated had been as *hairy* as Khaled. The male dancers she performed with had almost as little hair on their body as she did, and she had a regular appointment with the Bluebird's beautician and her little pot of pink wax.

'This makes me your first,' he said, with a great deal of satisfaction in that deep, dark Russian voice that made her hand shake.

'Yes, Khaled…' she'd give him that '…you're my first.'

He chuckled.

'Thirty degrees to the skin…perpendicular to the edge,' she muttered under her breath, and then she took the first stroke, running the blade up his throat.

Gratifyingly, only soapy hair fell away and no blood. *Yet*

'I still think you should have gone to a barber,' she murmured.

His dark eyes flashed to hers and held them. 'If you want the kill, your honour is the head.'

Gigi made a humming noise. 'I'm going to leave that one alone. It sounds too weird.'

He chuckled. 'I'm doing it for you—you should have the privilege.'

He was being incredibly patient with her, watching her face as she concentrated on the task, telling her he'd never seen a woman make so many grimaces in his life.

Finally she was done and he got up and thrust his face into the bucket of cold water, bringing his wet head up like a wild animal and shaking off the beaded residue.

Gigi stared at him in astonishment.

She was looking at a man she only half recognised. It unnerved her for a few seconds—perhaps because of the dream she'd been having since arriving in this strange place. In the dream she'd woken to an empty tower room. She called and called and when Khaled finally came up the steps he was a different man.

Silly. She gave a self-conscious laugh and reached up to stroke the clean sweep of his jaw. He grinned back at her. It really was Khaled. Just not as she'd ever seen him before.

The beard was gone, but so was something else—the weight in his eyes. And he was breathtaking.

If she'd thought it would render him more vulnerable she'd been wrong. The sweeping planes of his cheekbones and jaw lay fully visible; the clean, subtle lines of his lips and the strength of his chin gave him solidity. Sure, he was bleeding a little here and there, from her nicks and cuts, but it only added to his rugged appeal.

Now she knew why she'd clung to that idea of 'just sex'. Thrust it at him constantly like a shield and a sword to keep him from getting too close to the truth. Or maybe to keep her own feelings at bay. She'd tried so hard to 'be a guy' about it, but in the end she was just a woman, with not a lot of relationship history, trying to make sense of how to be with this man. This big, tough, complicated man. The kind of man older, wiser women would probably reconsider before scaling.

She hadn't hesitated.

'What is it, Gigi?'

He wasn't slow on the uptake. Any minute now he'd work it out.

She could feel his concern and it focussed her. 'I missed a bit on your upper lip,' she said huskily.

Trying to steady her hand, because she really didn't want to end the life of the only man she could see herself spending the rest of *her* life with, Gigi scraped carefully along his lip-line.

Then she was done. He was clean-shaven, and she was suddenly aware that he was looking at her as if he knew what he was about to say was going to hurt her.

Gigi wanted to stopper up his mouth, but she couldn't.

She couldn't do anything but look at him as he said, 'Gigi, there's something you need to know.'

It had been her confession earlier this afternoon that had landed a hammer-blow to his decision to keep the facts from her.

If he didn't tell her, and she found out from someone else, she might just start to hate him—and he didn't want that to happen with Gigi. Not with Gigi.

He looked down at her. 'Do you remember the resort my

company's building on Mt Elbrus? It needs a road and there's been some difficulty with permission.'

'Oh?'

'People aren't happy about it.'

'The local people seem relatively friendly.'

'The road traverses traditional grazing land. Nothing new gets built without clan approval.'

'And you need clan approval for the road?'

'Smart girl.'

'How will you get it?'

'That's where you come in.'

'You want me to help?'

And that was when Khaled knew he was going to hurt her.

'The day I brought you here I'd received a phone call that morning, letting me know the clan elders were willing to talk.'

She kept wiping the blade, nodding as he spoke.

'A few weeks before that I spoke to the head man here. He wanted to know why I didn't have a home here, why I wasn't married, where my children were—'

Gigi looked up with interest.

'And he told me if I respected their customs they would see it my way.'

She gave a nervous laugh. 'So when do I meet your wife and children?'

'It's you, Gigi. You're the custom I've respected.'

She went very still.

'The Moscow papers were reporting that I'd stolen you off the stage in Paris. The elders approved. I was given this meeting.'

A sudden gust of wind scythed the grass around them and the towel over Gigi's shoulder flapped away.

She didn't move an inch.

'You brought me here to win permission for your road?' Her voice sounded very small, hollow.

'I brought me here because I wanted to be with you,'

he said with passionate conviction because he knew now it was true, only to add slowly, 'and because it was politic for the road.'

Gigi stared past him.

'I had no idea this was going to be the result.' His voice was slightly hoarse as emotions he didn't recognise began to push up through his body.

'But once it was, you went ahead and did it anyway? Without asking me?'

'I didn't think it mattered that much, Gigi.'

Her eyes shot to his.

'I was wrong to do it.' He made a gesture towards taking hold of her but she backed away. 'I should never have brought you here.'

But Gigi wasn't listening. She was running.

She ran up the slope, the breath coming short and sharp from her lungs. She would have kept running if she'd had a choice, but there was nowhere to go.

She was stuck—in a strange, wild country with a stranger, wilder man.

Whom she was in love with.

She had waited on the hillside until she'd seen Khaled leave before she returned. It was only when she was inside, packing her few belongings, that her hand began to sting and she unfisted it to discover a nasty red welt across her palm from where she'd tightly held on to the razor.

She'd been so worried about cutting him, but in the end he'd been the one with the blade to her throat. She'd just been blinded by her own feelings and what she'd thought were the genuine feelings of the man sitting before her to notice.

He'd been the one to draw her blood.

Khaled had gone no further than halfway down to the village when he knew he couldn't do it.

He shut off the engine and sat in the truck, looking down

at the flat roofs and winding roads of the mountain pass where he'd been raised.

If he went down to that community hall there would be some macho posturing, the scratching of pens, and then he would get the signatures he needed. But for the rest of his life he would see Gigi's trust being shattered in front of him.

He'd have to find another way.

He started the engine, turned the truck and tore back up the hill.

He didn't know what he wanted with Gigi, but he knew it wasn't this.

Which was when he swung out of the truck and looked up.

The top of the tower caught the late-afternoon sun.

Unease settled on him.

He looked across the yard and his belly went cold.

The Jeep was gone.

Khaled's head was pounding. His stepfather had used the claim of love as his weapon of choice. He'd used it like a gun, and like any weapon it made a man weak, prey to the worst of his nature when things went wrong. As a grown man Khaled only carried a rifle when he went hunting, a situation in which he had a purpose, and he never fired without the knowledge of every available variable. He did not inflict needless suffering on an animal. Everything he did in life had a moral centre and was a choice.

He'd told himself he was not his stepfather.

He didn't deal in cruelty, and nor did he fashion weapons to turn upon others or himself.

He made the right choices.

Only then Gigi had come along. Gigi had burrowed under his skin. Nothing with Gigi had ever felt like a choice. It was inexplicable to him—this feeling—because it had never happened to him before.

He had no idea what to do about that.

And as he strode through Nalchik's airport, knocking over a plastic chair that got in his way, cutting through security as he forced his way into the passenger lounge, he was aware that he wasn't entirely in control any more.

Gigi was huddled in her oversized cardigan in the airport lounge, staring out at the blinking lights of a plane that wouldn't take off.

An hour. She wasn't sure how she would get through the wait so she took it minute by minute.

If she'd felt vulnerable alone in that tower of Balkar stone in the gorge, it was nothing to how she felt now—the only woman as far as she could see, with no luggage, no money, just her passport and the ticket Lulu had organised for her.

It was a far cry from the way she'd come here, wrapped in the luxury of Khaled's world, trusting as a lemming heading for the proverbial cliff.

She drew her knees up to her chin, thankful for the denim keeping her legs warm.

She glanced around and caught the gaze of two men sitting nearby. They hadn't been nearby five minutes ago. They'd shifted closer.

Gigi told herself not to be paranoid, but she wrapped her arms a little tighter around her knees.

She was perfectly safe.

An announcement was made in Russian.

Would she even know when her plane was going to take off?

She buried her face against her knees.

Heavy footsteps came ominously close and then stopped. Forcing herself to take a look, she lifted her head slowly.

Khaled was standing over her, in jacket and jeans, twice the size of the men who had been eyeing her up.

He was a wall no one was coming through.

That must be why relief was pounding through her. Now Khaled was here nothing bad would happen to her.

Even as the thought formed a fatal crack appeared in her logic.

Khaled *was* the bad thing.

'Gigi,' he said, and the urge to leap out of her seat and fling herself into his arms was almost overwhelming.

But she couldn't—not any more.

He was a liar. He'd lied to her. He'd used her. He cared only about his business interests. What had he said to her about the cabaret? *I'll replace you.* He'd only keep her in the role as long as she made it pay.

She held her ground.

'I've been out of my mind,' he said. 'I came home and found the Jeep gone. Then I got a call from the French Embassy, asking me to report to their consulate in Moscow tomorrow concerning my activities with an Irish national currently resident in France. That would be *you*, Gigi.'

He seemed angry, but it was anger held in restraint, and Gigi was also getting something else from him. A fierce sort of bewilderment. Crazily, a part of her wanted to take his hand and hold on.

It was what she'd been doing for the last couple of weeks.

But that wasn't possible any more.

She was so tired and cold, and just worn out from thinking in circles—no wonder she was fantasising like this…she just didn't know what to do.

'Lulu,' she said hoarsely. 'I rang her for my ticket. Her stepfather—'

'Is a French government official—so I have learned. So now I must take you home and restore you to your friends.'

'No, that's not what I want,' she began, leaping up. 'I can go home on my own two feet. I don't need you organising things for me any more.'

'But it is what I want.'

'What *you* want?' Gigi could barely look at him she was

so angry. 'That's all it is to you—what *you* want. What about *me*? What *I* want?'

'You got what you wanted, Gigi. L'Oiseau Bleu.'

If he'd punched her she couldn't have been more winded.

But suddenly she could look him in the eye. And she lifted her chin—because she'd learned in the hard school of Carlos Valente that you didn't stop taking the knocks until you couldn't get up any more.

'You knew I was falling in love with you. You can't have been blind to it. You used my feelings against me, for your own ends, and the joke is I would have helped you had you just *asked* me. You didn't. You chose instead to make a fool of me.'

'You don't love me, Gigi. Love is just another word for fear.'

'You think I'm *afraid*? You think I'm—what?—hiding behind the cabaret?'

'You won't try out for the Lido, Gigi, and as far as I'm aware that's the most prestigious joint in town. Why is that?'

'Because I'm loyal!' she hollered. 'Something *you* seem to have missed!'

'Loyal? You're scared.'

'No.'

She was shaking her head vigorously but she knew he could see she was weakening. She was backing away now. He'd almost pushed her backwards entirely.

He gave her another shove.

'And you're lying to yourself. This has always been about what I could do for you.'

'No.'

'Prove it,' he said. 'Make the choice. Me or the job.'

Suddenly Gigi wanted him to be that billionaire bastard he'd been written about as being.

But she knew better. She knew so much more about him.

She knew enough that she could feel her legs almost breaking under her with the weight of what he was doing to her.

Because if he cared for her he wouldn't put her love to a test.

She hadn't asked him to love her. She hadn't asked anything of him.

She looked at him sadly and shook her head.

'I want the job,' she said, swallowing hard on the fierce craving pushing up her throat, and she saw the flash of hard satisfaction cross his face and knew at last that what her instincts had been warning her of was true.

'Because there *is* no choice,' she said, almost to herself. 'You haven't given me a choice.'

As she turned away he tried to take her bag from her. For a moment she was thrown, almost thought he was going to stop her.

She wished in that moment that he would. A terrible, terrible wish.

But then she saw that he only wanted to hand it to his bodyguard, who had been hovering there the whole time.

She'd been so upset she hadn't even noticed.

'Grisha is flying with you to Moscow. End of discussion.'

She didn't argue because what was the point? He was always going to win.

And suddenly it was as if she was twelve years old again, and finally able to do that double somersault.

Carlos would be so proud of her—he'd have to love her. Or so she'd thought.

'*My daughter,*' he'd kept saying. '*My daughter is going to be the star attraction in this show.*'

But when she'd broken her collarbone and hadn't been able to perform it hadn't been Carlos who'd sat by her as she lay frightened and tearful in hospital.

The show has to go on.

She'd been all alone. Just as she was now.

She didn't let herself feel again until the plane was in

the air. By that time the aerial silks were cut and she was tumbling, tumbling…all her pretty tricks and turns lost to her now. All she could do was try to fall without breaking any bones.

Khaled boarded a helicopter and flew back to Moscow that same night.

He stormed into his apartment and the first thing he spotted was her shoe. Her little caramel boot, lying on its side beside his bed. He spent twenty full minutes hunting for its twin.

He never found it, but he did pull out a bottle of rot-gut vodka and proceed to get very, *very* drunk.

It was easier than facing what he'd done.

He'd seen what love did to people. How it failed you— when his father had died on his mother. How it twisted you—his stepfather's cruel jealousy. And how it weakened you—his own longing for comfort as a boy which had been beaten and kicked out of him, and then enabled him to make all of the tough decisions that had brought him to where he stood today: bloody but victorious in the Russian business bear pit.

Yes, he thought he had seen what love did to people— until he'd seen what he had done last night.

To Gigi.

To the woman he loved.

Because he *did* love her. How the hell could he *not* love her?

Yet even to imagine undoing those knots he'd tied tore at the weft and weave of the life he had put together. He had no idea what his life would look like if he undid them all. He suspected it wouldn't be pretty.

But Gigi had given him a glimpse of a *different* life. One which wasn't his, or hers, but *theirs*, and he was still under the influence of how strange and utterly beguiling it had looked.

On that last afternoon, as Gigi had run up the slope, her long back straight and her bare legs flashing through the grass, he had tried to imagine...

How it would feel to lose her.

How it would feel not to have her in his life any more.

He hadn't been able to get it out of his head.

And now he knew how bleak it actually was.

No light—just sounds. Even his Moscow apartment felt empty.

He'd literally built a fortress inside him. It was like the one he had taken Gigi to, but there was no illumination at the top of the tower that was his life. There was no moon and stars to gaze up at from their bed.

There was only fear and paranoia and the sound of his stepfather's fist banging on the door.

Two years ago Khaled had built up the interior of his real fortress in tandem with an architect and a designer. Made of Balkar stone, it had been standing for eight centuries against the immensity of the mountain. He'd known what he needed—space and light and warmth—two years before he had first laid eyes on Gigi Valente.

Khaled suspected that from the moment he'd looked up and caught his first glimpse of a bright-haired alluring fairy he'd known he'd been laying the ground for her. He'd won her cabaret in a lucky hand of poker. If that wasn't fate he didn't know what was.

She'd tumbled into his life and he should have caught her.

The next morning brought him the mother of all headaches—a sort of drilling in his skull that he endured stoically because he deserved every bit of suffering he could visit upon himself.

He showered and shaved and put on a suit.

He had to get her back. But first he needed a plan.

CHAPTER SIXTEEN

GIGI'S SKIN FELT CLAMMY, her limbs weak, as she stumbled into Arrivals at Orly after several hours in the air.

Probably the flu, she decided dully.

She saw Lulu coming towards her. She looked like a snowman in a white puffy jacket. Only Lulu could look attractive in that much puff. Pink fur framed her face and her dark curls were frothing about merrily. Her smile faded as she took in Gigi's appearance.

I must look awful, thought Gigi tiredly.

'Oh, God,' said Lulu, stopping a few feet in front of her, 'what have I done?'

'I don't know,' she whispered hoarsely, 'but can we save it for later?'

Her best friend took charge as only Lulu could, nabbing them a cab immediately as several drivers swarmed Lulu's barely raised hand.

Gigi laid her head in Lulu's lap as the taxi took off.

'Are you sure it's flu?' Lulu was asking anxiously.

'That or travel sickness. Let me sleep, Lu. I feel so tired.'

She stirred some time after they'd hit the stop-start traffic of inner Paris.

As the taxi climbed the hill Gigi wound down the window.

'Stop here,' she told the driver.

'What are you doing?' Lulu called after her.

Gigi staggered from the cab and made her way to the central strip. She stood there staring up at L'Oiseau Bleu. Sure enough, it was boarded up.

A top-tier architectural restoration firm responsible for many sites around the city had its signage plastered everywhere.

Lulu reached her side and hovered.

'Don't hate me, Gigi. I didn't tell you that part because I

wanted you to come home. I know I was wrong. But I was scared something would happen to you.'

When Gigi didn't answer Lulu sniffled.

'The rumour is he's put up fifteen million euros.'

Gigi shook her head.

'Please forgive me, Gigi.' Lulu began to sob. 'I didn't realise.'

Struggling out of the grip of her depression, Gigi turned to her friend. '*What* didn't you realise?'

'That you love him.'

It moved through her like sunlight.

'Well, of *course* I love him, you eejit—I loved him from the moment he washed my feet!'

Lulu was still crying in earnest, and Gigi wrapped her arms around her best friend's shoulders.

'I didn't come home because he shut the Bluebird down, Lu. I came home because he's given me a job.'

Lulu gave a sniff. 'What sort of job?' she asked suspiciously.

'You're talking to the new manager of L'Oiseau Bleu.'

Lulu dropped her handbag. 'You're the *what*?'

Despite everything. Gigi found it in herself to laugh—even if it was a watery one. She bent down and handed Lulu's bag to her.

'Oh, Lord, if even *you* don't believe it I haven't got a chance with anyone else.'

Lulu dabbed at her nose with her wrist. 'It's not that I don't believe you, but of all things... You must be so happy, Gigi!'

'I—I am.'

Only she wasn't happy, and from the way Lulu was looking at her—had been looking at her since her arrival—her misery was plain to see.

She hadn't known how miserable she was until this moment. It was like being drenched with a bucket of cold water

She wasn't happy, and no amount of telling herself that this was her dream come true was going to change the fact that what mattered more to her than the realisation of her dreams for the theatre, more than the knowledge that the jobs of her friends were safe—more even than doing something to preserve the memory of her mother—was telling Khaled that she loved him. She loved him in all the ways a woman could love a man.

Only all that mattered to him in the end was himself. His comfort, his financial success, having all of it *his* way.

That night as she lay alone in her bed, rendered cold and narrow and not like hers at all, she couldn't sleep. She climbed out of bed and went to her window. She could see the corner of the theatre's peaked roof further down the hill. That old theatre held so many of her childhood dreams, but it didn't hold her attention as it once had.

She looked up into the sky, unmarked by pollution on this cold winter's night, and wondered if Khaled was looking up at the same wedge of moon and sprinkling of stars in that fearsomely clean sky over the gorge. Was he thinking of her? Was he remembering how it had felt to lie in that cot of marmot furs, sharing body heat and stories? Was he thinking about how good it had felt to fall asleep like that? Was he thinking about her at all?

'He thought you were Rita when we all *know* you're Katharine Hepburn. So you got burned.'

Susie said this so pragmatically Gigi couldn't be offended. But then, she'd made an art form of not being offended. Until Khaled had torn the blinders off her eyes.

'Rita?' Adele frowned.

'Hayworth. Married all those larger-than-life men who disappointed her one way or the other.'

'Khaled virtually *gave* her the cabaret to manage—that's not a disappointment,' said Leah, but everyone stared at her until she hung her head.

The girls had turned up at the theatre this afternoon to

stick their noses in. As long as they wore hard hats that wasn't a problem on-site.

But as Gigi walked away with Lulu she said, 'He *did* give this cabaret to me, and that makes me the lowest common denominator.'

Lulu screwed up her nose. 'The what?'

'I'm the lowest common denominator,' Gigi said desultorily. 'He gave it to me because I slept with him.'

'I don't think anyone makes a fortune with bad business decisions, Gigi. He clearly thinks you're capable.'

That was the nicest thing Lulu had ever said about Khaled, and it had a ring of truth.

Gigi stood in her hard hat as the carpenters swung hammers overhead and dust rose from the curtains every time something got shifted on the stage.

This wasn't her usual environment, although in the past four weeks she had learned to read the builder's plans—well, she could make sense of where they were putting the toilets. Her real role was organising the talent. She'd already lined up a choreographer and costumier for the new show, which was far more up her alley than chip dust and power saws.

Only today she'd got a message to say they were bringing in the flooring and wanted her to approve the colour.

'He's doing this for *you*,' Lulu insisted, looking around.

Gigi flinched. 'Do you mind if we don't talk about him any more?'

Lulu eyed her nervously. 'Sure. Only he's standing over there.'

For a few beats it had sounded as if Lulu had said, *He's standing over there*… Which was when she turned around and…

Gigi almost dropped her clipboard.

Lulu evaporated like smoke—along with the workmen, the noise, the past few weeks.

He filled all her available vision and everything else was reduced to the horizon.

She took a step towards him. Stopped. He looked different. He'd cut his hair, and although he remained clean shaven there was stubble. He wore a suit.

She hated suits. But maybe it was better to see him like this. *As he was.* A ruthless businessman with his own agenda.

Only the eyes that met hers were not those of a businessman.

They were hot—and starved.

He stepped out of the gloom and into the light and the dust motes.

She wouldn't be surprised if he was just a figment of her imagination.

Then, 'Gigi…' he said. His voice was low and rough… and so familiar.

She pulled herself together. There would be no fainting at his feet on *her* watch.

Gigi was highly aware that this was approximately the spot where she'd landed at his feet just a few weeks ago.

Given the cabaret was now a shell around them, and the place looked as if a bomb had gone off, it was somehow appropriate.

He'd hit her life like a meteor, and if L'Oiseau Bleu was in the process of transformation she could be said to be too.

Only Gigi didn't hold by all that hokum. She had always been capable—she just hadn't been given the means by which to bring things off.

'You're cutting it fine,' he said, in that dark, roughened voice, stepping towards her.

Six weeks and that was what he said to her?

'On the contrary,' she said, and her voice only shook a little bit, 'we're ahead of schedule.'

'The press conference, Gigi. It's in an hour.'

'I'm not going to that.'

'I'm afraid it's in your contract. You *did* read your contract, didn't you?'

'I read enough.' He was so close now she had to tilt back her head.

Actually, she hadn't read anything—but she had used a lawyer, and she knew there was something about media appearances in it, but until now hadn't made that link.

Why on earth would anyone want to hear from *her*?

'You should have had a closer look at what you signed on for.'

She didn't respond.

He was looking at her with the strangest look in his eyes and giving her all the wrong messages again.

'I'll drive you over.'

Every kind of refusal was on her lips, but what came out was an exasperated, 'All right.'

He didn't touch her as he walked her out into the street, but she could feel him—and it was a special kind of wonderful torture.

In the bright daylight she could see there was a grey tinge to his skin. He didn't look well.

'Have you been ill?' She had to ask.

'Flu,' he said, and shrugged, all the while holding her with his eyes.

'Me too,' she mumbled, and then noticed the limo hovering.

'Not the Spyder today,' he said, as if reading her mind. 'I wanted to talk to you.'

'About my job?'

'No, Gigi, about us.'

She began to shake. She couldn't look at him.

She shook her head. 'No, no, no…' And kept walking.

'Gigi! Be fair!'

Somewhere she found it in herself to shout, 'Life's not fair, Khaled! I'm going home to change. I guess I'll see you at the press conference.'

* * *

There was no way she was climbing into the back of that car with him.

Everyone would talk.

She couldn't bear it—not when she'd made a little progress over the last month or so. She might not have everyone's respect, but she had their co-operation and that was a start. She told herself she wasn't risking that by hopping in and out of limos with their billionaire boss.

Gigi went home and took a quick shower, and she almost put on her version of a suit she wore to most meetings when her eye was caught by the white and scarlet frock she'd picked up on a whim under Lulu's influence in a vintage clothing sale.

She had it on and her hair swept up when Lulu walked in.

'You are *so* not wearing that to the press conference?'

But Lulu sounded thrilled.

'Yes, I am,' said Gigi, knowing now what Lulu meant when she said that some days the right frock was the only thing that stood between you and despair.

Well, only vintage Givenchy was going to hold her together this afternoon.

'In that case,' said Lulu resolutely, 'we all will.'

The press conference was being held in a reception room on the ground floor of a luxury hotel.

Half of Paris seemed to have turned up, and the audience had spilled over into the lobby. The hum of preparation and the sound of chairs being shifted ceased as the doors swept open and the Bluebirds arrived *en masse*.

Gigi led them, in their showy old-time frocks: twenty-four glamour girls lined up in a row.

Clicking cameras responded.

'It's like something straight out of Fashion Week,' said one journalist.

'No, it's called making an old-time entrance,' said another.

Gigi indicated the need for chairs for the other twenty-three dancers and as she took her own identified where Khaled was in the room.

She sat with her girls and glared at him.

'Ladies and gentlemen...'

One of the suits launched into the press release.

Questions erupted.

Gigi listened to Khaled answer all the questions in that same deep voice that had haunted her dreams for six awful weeks.

She tried not to stare too long at him, but he was magnetic, charming the pants off all the females in the room with that quiet Russian drawl.

Although she knew now he wouldn't be taking advantage of that particular skill. He wasn't that man at all.

He was *her* man.

Only he didn't want to be.

'Why have you chosen to do this, Mr Kitaev?'

'Some people have called this your love letter to Paris. Is there any truth in that?'

Khaled leaned forward, his eyes focussed on her, and said in that low, deeply accented voice, 'It's my love letter to a particular woman.'

He had clearly gone off-script, because the suits looked alarmed and there was a flurry of hands raised as everyone vied to ask the next question, given the answer to that one wasn't in the information sheet.

'What's her name?'

'Is she French?'

'Is she a Bluebird?'

Gigi struggled to understand his meaning. She wanted to leap to her feet and demand to know exactly who he was sending love letters to when he'd told her love didn't even exist!

There was a low murmur among the girls, and a rustle of

skirts, and Gigi suddenly became aware that twenty-three
mascara-laden pairs of eyes were glued to her.

Khaled gave the cameras the half-smile that had caused
all this trouble to begin with and said directly, 'She's Irish.
She *is* a Bluebird. She's the reason I've moved heaven and
earth to have you all here today. Exactly six weeks from
the day she first dropped so fatefully into my life. She's the
person two million Parisians have to thank for saving their
cabaret.'

Adele drummed her feet enthusiastically. Susie gave a
thumbs-up, and Leah looked so sour her drooping mouth
might drop off.

Gigi only knew this afterwards—when Lulu filled her
in—because at that very moment she couldn't take her eyes
off the man telling the world—well, what *was* he telling
the world?

'My last visit to Paris was the most memorable of my
life, because I met the woman I want to spend the rest of
my life with.'

The cameras exploded in a flurry that sounded like ap-
plause.

Gigi didn't know she was on her feet until she was halfway out through the side door.

'Gigi!'

She heard him call her name, but didn't wait to find out
why.

Khaled scraped back his chair.

There was another flurry of questions, but he didn't hear
a word as he shouldered his way out of the reception room.

Gigi was exiting through the entrance doors when he exploded out into the lobby.

She was on the avenue outside, getting into a taxi, when
he hit the pavement. He saw the flash of her skirts and began
to run.

He grabbed the door as she went to shut it and jumped
in alongside her.

'Get out of my taxi!'

He gave the driver an address in Montmartre.

Gigi folded her arms. 'I'm *not* sharing this taxi with you.

She was, he thought, the most amazing girl, with her hands balled into fists, looking ready to belt him one. But her eyes gave her away, and they made him feel...made him feel...

Khaled gave a groan of sheer frustrated happiness and pulled her forward into his arms.

She went. But she was rigid, and she fought against him a little, and dipped her head so he couldn't kiss her. He understood, because she needed words, and he was struggling to find the ones that would make sense of the enormous reservoir of feeling he had stored up these last week without her.

Because there had never been any doubt for him: from first sight she had been the one.

After all, she'd thrown herself off a tank, turned up at his hotel, had herself papped as if they were Jagger and Faithful back in the day *and* let him lock her up in a tower.

They were stories to tell their grandchildren. Because there *would* be grandchildren, after a tribe of children—a family he would build with her. A home...

But all he wanted right now was to be where he was: in the back of this taxi, holding her in his arms and knowing she was safe and sound and would be his, as he was hers. *I* he could find those damn words.

'Bastard,' she said.

That wasn't the right word, but from Gigi's soft lips it was a kiss.

'I love you,' he said, holding her strong yet fragile body against him. 'I've loved you from the moment I saw you on that stage floor. I've missed you every moment of every day I should never have let you go. And if I want to give you a cabaret as a gift I damn well will and Paris can go hang.'

They might have been the words she wanted, but she gave him a hard shove in the chest all the same. 'You made me choose between you and the theatre.'

'Have them both—have it all.' He kissed her in between promises. Her temples, her eyelids, her nose, her mouth. 'Never again, *malenki*. You do not leave me ever again.'

Given she was kissing him back, with damp, tear-salty lips, the ground beneath his feet began to feel more solid.

They sailed up the hill without either of them really noticing, until the driver was tapping on the window. Khaled got out and gave her his hand.

'Where are we?'

It was a pretty narrow street at the top of the hill. There was a house with cream walls and square windows behind a high stone wall.

He drew her by the hand into the rambling garden behind the wall.

'The ten-kilometre rule,' he said, locking the gate behind them.

'What…?' she choked.

'You once told me you had a rule about the men you dated—they couldn't live outside a ten-kilometre radius of Montmartre. So I bought a house within your exclusion zone.'

'A house? But you live in Moscow.'

'Here…there. I can run everything from my phone—or so you tell me. It's a little smaller than the cabaret, but it's big enough. For us. For any children we have.'

A slow smile began to blossom on her lips.

Which was when he knew those were the words they both wanted.

Gigi looked up at him. Something wonderful was happening inside her. Everything was opening up and she felt love pouring through her like an elixir.

Khaled stood four-square in front of her, a wall that nothing was getting over, through or around. *Her wall*.

He framed her face.

'Marry me, Gigi. Have children with me. Grow old with me.'

In response Gigi wrapped her arms around his neck, and he pulled her against him and proceeded to kiss her passionately, thoroughly, and without much respect for the garden and its bed of long, soft grasses.

Several of which Gigi was plucking out of her hair as they ambled, arms entwined, down the road at twilight back to her flat. Below the rooftops of Montmartre glittered and deep shadows sprang up to cast everything in a mysterious heady glow.

* * * * *